Large Format Paper Edition
Continuous Printing
First Published December 1, 2023
Release 2.142 February 6, 2025

ISBN: 9780983857518

Published by

WEST WINTER PRESS

Sky Valley, California, USA

Sexual Content Advisory and Promise:

This book contains expansive and explicit depiction of lovemaking with passion and consent.

Andrés + Mila

A Sexual Account
By John Kirnan

About Andrés + Mila

In 2016, I published my novel "The White Sky" under the pen name John Caedan. The first month of the love affair of Andrés and Mila transpires in it, a tale of artists pursuing an entanglement of the heart and body with everything at stake.

I published the 36 episodes of their lovemaking as a separate volume, this one. I primarily intend it as a "pillow book," meant to delight and ignite a couple as they read an episode to each other ... or for any other healthy purpose our sexual souls might desire.

It might seem to be "too much." Relentless. I suggest thinking of each episode as a lyric poem or a "short!" Read one. Close the book. Only open again when it becomes impossible to keep your hands off.

I hope to interest readers in the narrative in which these episodes are embedded. If this happens to you, please consider reading "The White Sky."

John Kirnan

jjkirnan.com

TheWhiteSky.com
JohnCaedan.com

Contents

chapter 1

a thousand times

Friday, May 23, 2014
3:14 a.m.

From The White Sky: **In the night, Mila executes a
sculpture, with Andrés as model. They have known each
other for 12 hours, with sexual sparks flying. Then, he
challenges her:**
"Mila."
"What?"
*"Why is it your mission to sculpt a man who loves
women?"*
*She returns to fussing with the coffee preparation, not
looking up from it. He walks to her at the gas stove and
twists off the burner under the water. The sound of the
snap jolts the room. He reaches for her.*
"Not now," she says, and casts her body against his.

With shrieks of pleasure, Mila goes off, first by his
hand, then his mouth, a woman magnificent with
sexual joy. Now she lies on her back, descending, each
breath a sigh like the word *yes.* Andrés lies face down,
senses filled with the scent and taste of Mila, hip
pressing hers, hot for his turn. Just as he stirs to take it,
she rotates onto her belly, pulls knees up and under,
arches her back, bottom rising high. This ballet sends
him white-hot behind the eyes.

M: "Please."

Andrés moves behind. She tilts up further, thighs
separating.

M: "Here."

His urge leaps. The entry, one power stroke.

M: "Oh oh oh oh oh."

First time in Mila.

The sensation of *having* rushes through. Having her. It thrills his organs, the physical organs and those of the numinous sexual self. To *have* her.

He slides out.

She twists at the waist and looks over her shoulder, right in his eyes. Her fingers caress the flesh between thighs to quicken it for pleasure. The sound of wet flesh slithering lights his mind.

M: "Please."

A: "Move your hands."

Mila splays both hands face down on the bed, fingers shiny with juice. He positions between the lips. She steadies her bottom. She is so open, so ready, his breathing stops in awe. Andrés thrusts in, thudding all the way deep, groaning, thick with satisfaction, the world succulent and ripe.

M: "Oh no oh no oh no."

Andrés begins his strokes.

M: "You made me scream."

His penetrations accelerate.

M: "Your mouth on me. I love to scream."

Her words infuriate his drive. The sight of lips forced apart by cock – fat lips all swollen – his thrusts grow fierce. Her pelvis adjusts after each stroke to be perfect for the next, swiveling hips to deliberately take penetration, to aim her body best for slick entry. This is thrilling.

Salacious talk, flung it at him while peering over her shoulder, one word on each thrust …

M: "Yes, more, more, deep, more, more, in, in, in. In. Hard. Hard. Hard."

She shifts again, spreading thighs a fraction more – to expose the fucking hotrod center of a woman. Into the juicy core of it he slams home his thrusts, grunting, braying … twenty, thirty, fifty times. Her sex remains perfectly tilted to take all.

Fire races up his spine.

His roar fills the studio.

"Grrphff." Emptying, spilling, spraying.

Mila coos sweetly, a giggle of girl-happiness for giving herself like a woman. She uncoils flat onto the mattress, straightening her legs. Andrés collapses on her back, moaning, staying in, throbbing with aftershocks. She wiggles under his weight.

M: "Crush me."

He sinks on her frame until close to smothering. She squirms. Fighting it. Resisting.

M: "Crush me."

He releases his weight off one elbow. She screams into the sheets.

Finally, Mila twists around, throwing him off. Jerks of release continue to rack his body. Arms around his neck, she presses her front to his.

They soak in the sweaty afterness.

They do not speak while he catches up with breaths. A carnal scent floats in the bed. Eventually they drift to rest.

This is how it will be with Mila.

He wants her a thousand times.

M: "I can't believe you held back like that. You made me come first. Twice. Why didn't you just spread me open and do me fast, right away, like most boys would?"

A: "Do me?"

M: "Fuck me. You're okay with that word?"

A: "Yes."

M: "Because I don't like to use if for ugly. Only for fun."

A: "I'm okay with that word for it. There's no better one."

M: "We don't mean anything hurtful or cruel with it, okay? Or crude."

A: "To fuck each other is beautiful."

M: "Dirty-beautiful."

A: "We make that word sweet."

M: "Why didn't you fuck me right away?"

A: "The sound of screaming and moaning – I wanted to hear it. I crave it. It gets me going. And the taste of it …"

M: "Me first? Just this time, or …?"

A: "Every."

M: "Wait a second, wait a second, I want to write that down. I'm going to make you sign it."

A: "I'll sign."

M: "You'll make me come first, every time?"

A: "Yes. At least once, first, every time."

M: "Andrés, I love your fucking mouth!"

A: "That is so sweet."

They laugh, each safe to let the other *see in* after orgasm.

A: "Mila, your words? Talk while I'm in you. Talk like that. Say things. It made me boil over."

M: "Dirty talk or sweet talk?"

A: "Both."

chapter 2

heavenly ice cream

Friday, May 23, 2014
10:14 p.m.

*From The White Sky: Andrés rolls up to the studio at
10:15 p.m. Emerging from the car, he moves
confidently to the small porch and entryway. Mila's
form fills the doorway. Unexpected gentleness overtakes
them as they walk to the side of the bed. There, arms
wrap around, heads tilt opposite, bodies press – and a
kiss arises, as sweet as homecoming, yet immodest with
carnal need.*

A kiss that does not hurry. It surges lightly, one
languorous wave receding while the next crests above it.
His hands cradle her head. The vibrations of her body
say *yes*, with torso bending and hips swaying.

How long do Andrés and Mila kiss?

Does a kiss end when their mouths separate and he
says, 'I want to feel your breasts against me' and one
unbuttons the shirt of the other and then the other the
other's and then her arms encircle his neck to pull him
tight and press soft hard to him and lips touch again and
slide against lips? Is that the next kiss or the previous,
still?

At the end of the kissing, clothing drops to the floor
where they stand next to the bed. Mila sinks to her knees
on the pile.

Gentleness. Soft mouth on hard sex, sliding it
partway in, only the lightest of pressure, wet pressure.
Her lips form up under the rim and hold steady, mouth
full of wet, letting the tip bathe. She rotates and tilts,
makes the head swivel in the slipperiness. Only the tip
in, although he tries for more. He wants to thrust.

A: "Let me."

She releases and looks up into his eyes.

M: "I like it just in a little like that. Just the head. It's like a French kiss. But you want it deep, don't you?

A: "Yes."

M: "Cock all the way in."

A: "Yes."

M: "Let me do it. Hold still."

A: "Yes."

He closes his eyes.

Her mouth slips over the tip, wetter than ever. Then, with exquisite grace and gentleness, she leans forward and takes the length.

His voice rings around the room. His knees buckle. He barely remains standing. Mila holding steady … then her jaw relaxes and opens with surrender. She eases forward another inch, and the tip penetrates the back of her throat – soft and magical, like heavenly ice cream melting. He cries out again.

Twice Mila slides off, twice her mouth fits to him and slides the shaft in … then … lets the tip all the way deep. She has made a cave of sublime wet softness slicked for penetration. On the last, the slowest, she takes it deepest, rotating her head to ease it down her throat. She grows still, impaled, surrendered and peaceful. To Andrés, infinity has opened under him, with every urge rushing into the impossible void.

Andrés puts his hands under her arms and draws her off and up. Mila squeals in surprise. They stand apart, staring at each other. Her lips, chin, and breasts shine in the low light.

M: "You could slide in my mouth a hundred times. I would love that. Don't you want to?"

A: "No. Get in the bed. Offer your other mouth."

She strokes her neck slowly with expressive hands.

M: "Right here, Andrés. Your cock down my throat. Right down it. It makes my heart race, feeling it go deep. I'll take you in my mouth."

A: "On the bed."

She folds onto the mattress, elongating, face up, and slides both hands down between her legs.

M: "It makes me wet right here. You cock in my throat makes me wet."

She opens the lips with her fingers, slips up and down the pouty lips, and one finger hooks in to pull out juice.

M: "Fuck me."

Andrés slides between her legs and makes the penetration. Face to face, they find the sweet rhythm. The hot idea floats between them – each thrust might be in her mouth just as well.

M: "In my mouth, anytime."

Andrés doubles down on the penetration he wants. The confidence in it fills his chest with fiery certainty. Indomitable. The woman below can only grunt and squeal as his power goes home.

Twice in ten minutes the pressure in Mila's pelvis explodes. The sound of her second ignites his thunder, thrusting his organ deep while she quivers, helpless in release.

All during, Mila seldom lets him look in her eyes, but when he steals a glance, he makes sure she catches every ounce of male pride to have won a woman who would let him do these things to her.

the girl-melting

Saturday, May 24, 2014
1:30 a.m.

From The White Sky: Mila describes her satisfaction, and then asks Andrés to 'be more aggressive.' They establish consent. He asks for a safe word. She says, "my safe word is time out." Instantly, he leaps over the table and drags her screaming and laughing to the floor of the studio.

A: "Enough of this floor."

Andrés' mouth is slick from taking the juices between her thighs. This fount is effusive, with sprinkling of liquids everywhere. The walls of the studio are ringing from her screams of pleasure in orgasm.

He draws himself up, bends at the knees, lifts her frame with a hold under hips. She wraps around him horizontally, like a belt circling his waist, cinched by her hands grasping behind knees. She makes no sound while he stomps across the studio into the bed alcove. He tosses her on the bed face down, jumps in, pushes her legs apart and thrusts in.

No moan no screech no swear.

A: "Scream it out."

M: "No."

Four, five, ten power strokes from behind. Not a sound.

A: "Scream your screams."

M: "No."

He stops. He is in – and blocked – a clench of muscles refuses him full possession.

A: "Let go."
M: "No."
He pulls out, spins around and straddles her at the waist. Using elbows, he wedges her thighs apart, grasps her bottom with both hands, squeezes and pushes the flesh. This kneading does not overcome resistance in her pelvis – he senses it as a tangible wall of stubborn denial. She tries twice to roll over – he restrains her face down.
A: "Put your hands between your legs."
Her fingers appear from under, along the inside of her thighs.
A: "Touch the lips."
Each index finger eases into place.
A: "Cross your hands."
She complies, which makes the angle of touching better. He watches her fingers tease and caress.
A: "Pull the lips open. Push some fingers in."
Her hands uncross and fingers disappear, one from each hand. Mila eases herself open, gradually reaching deeper, gathering the silky flesh.
A: "I'm going to pull you wide."
M: "No. No more."
A: "When I do, push your fingers in. As deep as you can."
M: "No."
A: "I know your legs can open more. I can feel it."
M: "I don't want to."
A: "Now."
He pulls the round mounds apart. Her legs spread another two inches. Her hands ease out, reform with two fingers each gathered at the opening, then slide and slither into vagina.
She cannot stop a plaintive moan escaping her throat. Fingers withdraw, then penetrate again, hands glistening when they emerge each time. The sight of her wide open, caressing in the wet, makes him burn.
A: "... the hot spot in there."
M: "It's not for you."

A: "Then touch it with your fingers. I'll hold your hips apart like this and watch you touch it."

M: "Oh, oh, oh."

She coos under his instruction. Her hands roll the succulent flesh. She sinks deep, seeking the core – the psychic nexus of the yoni.

M: "Oh oh oh oh."

Since she has already been ravaged to orgasm by his mouth -- Mila is not far from coming again.

A: "Go all the way."

M: "Oh, oh ... Oh."

Mila's fingers inside the stretched-open sex, and the ones underneath on her outside spot, bring swelling, throbbing, and after more, more, more stroking, set her off into a muscle-clenching explosion. She has blasted herself into orbit. Face-down in the bed, she screams with no inhibition, agonized screams of joy that do not sound like pain.

He does not let her coast. Spinning off, around, and behind, he fits into position, pulls her hands out, splits the lips apart with the head of his organ and thrusts hard, true, and fully in.

Still Mila resists, blocks the deep inside. He pulls out, leverages his hips, and pistons in.

M: "No, oh no. No. No."

A: "Fucking yes."

Suddenly her screams catch in her throat – frozen silence when she should have bellowed. Yet she is coming. Coming into the silent void, body arched in rigid suspension. His next three thrusts slam into the core chamber she has denied him – which she can no longer protect. On the fourth, the most powerful, her pent-up pressure spills out in a deafening scream, a new orgasm folding into the unfinished previous, with another gathering yet deeper. His assault has won the exquisite surrender, the girl-melting.

Andrés gives no heed. A woman is open under him. He

holds possession, as requested and claimed. Into the unprotected chamber of femme he penetrates hard, masterfully, with total abandon, just as he wishes. Not a thing in the time-in world can ever, will ever, not ever, prevent his thousands and thousands of strokes, each as rich as the next.

   When he reaches his last thrust, bellowing from the gut and splashing her insides, Mila is still grunting, quivering, and flooding beneath.

chapter 4

by hot consent

Saturday, May 24, 2014

4:00 a.m.

From The White Sky: A few hours after their consenting rough sex, Andrés and Mila open a bottle of scotch and recline entwined on an old couch in the middle of her art studio. They are mellow.

They kiss for an hour. Perhaps more. Confident lovers can do it. Slow and sensual, and sometimes outrageously liquid, gentle in play, to contrast with previous drama and fierce combats. Their mouths taste of scotch whiskey, and each other.

They change positions occasionally. When Mila is on top, her mouth sinks down into his. She knows how to signal for control, to make him relax and receive, and she explores his inside sensitivities. Her kisses are not always wet, nor always deep. Sometimes they are.

Flipping her around and under, Andrés rests the length of his right arm against her torso, the hand fitting under her chin, caressing her neck, easing her head back and forth. His kissing becomes aggressive and gentle by turns. After minutes of this she pulls her mouth away.

M: "Your arm between my breasts ... it presses against them when you move your hand on my neck ... that's a fresh move."

A: "It's how a shy boy works his way up to taking them in his hand."

M: "Yes. To go for second base. He should ask his girlfriend for each base."

They laugh at their half-inebriated teenage talking – inside their full-grown lovers' souls. Now they will play it as virgin first sex.

M: "Do they have the bases in Argentina?"

A: "I know them. American girls taught me. I like them all. Especially *un jonrón.*"

M: "Wait, is that what I think it is?"

A: "Home run."

M: "Ask for each thing. No stealing the bases."

A: "He doesn't want to ask. He wants to be that boy who keeps going for more."

M: "Americans call that 'proceed until apprehended'."

A: "I'll be an American in two years."

M: "Tonight, he should ask first. She's a virgin."

A: "He's rounding first and can't be stopped."

Andrés moves his hand down from her neck. Before it slips inside her shirt, she stops it with one of hers.

M: "No, Andrés. I love when you take without asking, I love that so much, but just for tonight, ask for each thing. The opposite, okay? To tease for fun. So I can say no a lot, and stop you. Like a young girl would. A virgin girl. Please?"

It would be adorable for her to say 'no' a lot.

A: "Let me open your shirt."

M: "Yes."

He laughs and begins to unbutton.

M: "When a girl allows a boy to open her blouse, and she has nothing underneath, that's letting him have sex."

A: "It's sex?"

M: "Almost. She's right on the edge of giving sex to a boy."

A: "Just by unbuttoning like this?"

M: "Yes. If that's as far as they go, she can tell her mamma they didn't have sex, but they really did have sex, because of bare breasts. Now tease me. I'm your modest virgin girlfriend and not letting you touch them for two months."

To obey, he does not push the garment aside, rather exposes a narrow strip of skin down the center. He resumes kissing her mouth, holding his left hand behind her neck and the edge of his right forearm lightly pressing her torso. Gradually, with skill, his arm's rocking motions begin to spread open the shirt.

M: "No! I didn't say you could do that. If you keep doing that my breasts will be bare, but you didn't ask."

A: "How long do I have to kiss you before you'll let me?"

M: "Never, unless you ask. You have to ask for each thing, and kiss me a lot in between."

A: "Just because I touch them, that doesn't mean you have to go all the way."

A giggle.

M: "Oh, we're not going all the way. With your hands on my breasts, that's sex. But I won't let you fuck me."

A: "What?"

M: "I won't let you fuck me, this is just a kissing date."

A: "What kind of virgin talks like that? With her filthy mouth?"

M: "A girl who wants to be pure but actually wants to be fucked."

A: "Let me hold them in my hand."

M: "No."

A: "Damn! Well, you're letting me French kiss a long time."

M: "Yes, you can kiss me all wet and everything, but if your hands touch my breasts, that's sex."

A: "Really?"

M: "No *jonrón* on this date. You can put your mouth inside mine as long as you want to."

He sets out to change her mind. Neck kisses, open mouthed and wet. Hand on her exposed abdomen gently stroking. Her breathing heats up – he feels the cool jolt of triumph – she is going to let him.

His right leg, bent at the knee, insinuates between her thighs little by little, until his ankle reaches the desirable vee, protected by jeans. Somehow, he gets away with this maneuver without asking.

A: "You can rub against that."

He presses the hard knob on the side of his ankle up into

the conjunction.

M: "No."

A: "Rub your beautiful cunny against it."

M: "No. Are you crazy?"

A: "Right through your jeans. Rub it against me."

M: "No sex."

A: "It's what a good boyfriend does you squeeze against it and I'll hold rock steady and you'll rub and rub and you'll get all wet in your jeans but it's not that I 'got in your pants' so you are still pure and you'll finish like that but it doesn't count as official sex and you don't have to lie to your mother."

M: "Oh my God. No, I can't. It's too bold."

He takes the edge of her shirt in his fingers, one side at a time, and pulls across, catching the rounded inside curve under it, bulging the flesh.

M: "I said no."

A: "Not bare if I stop there. Sometimes you wear a shirt with your curves exposed a little."

M: "That's to tease you. Teen girls do that."

A: "Ah, yeah, I know."

M: "Kiss me. If I put my tongue in your mouth while we're kissing, that's when you can put your hand in there."

A: "Where?"

M: "In there."

A: "Say it."

M: "French kiss. Lure me to put my tongue in your mouth. When I do, that's my signal you can touch my breasts."

For ten minutes she does not get lured. Soft tongues touch, but always inside her mouth. She sucks ardently. He withdraws. He holds her mouth open with his lips, but no more. An invitation. They hang in the silent kiss for precious moments, mouths sealed and open, the caves of dark-cherry dreams.

The instant he feels the tip of her tongue shyly searching inside his mouth, he slides his right hand under the shirt and touches tenderly. As he knew would happen, a deep groan wells up in her throat. He loves her tongue inside his mouth. He loves his hand cupping the rounded flesh.

When his mouth slips down to move her shirt aside completely, she squirms against it.

A: "Let me put the tips of them in my mouth."

M: "No."

A: "Grrr ..."

M: "Wait ... yes. Put them in your mouth. But no more. No more. This is too bold."

It only takes a few minutes with the nipples pulled into erection by his kisses for her hips to slip along the couch, thighs to open, and the hardness of his ankle to smash against the vee between them. She wraps around. She squeezes. The knob of his ankle goes home. In a moment the jeans are wet, right there.

So it goes, playfully. He is granted each advance through polite requests. She says no to each one at least twice before giving in. He rounds the bases.

Their clothes come off. She is wearing oh-so-sexy under-bottoms. With his cock rubbing the lips of her sex through the cloth – by hot consent – he can barely speak.

A: "Let me."

M: "Let you what?"

A: "Let me in."

M: "No. You can't put it in me."

A: "I'll be gentle and slow."

M: "I said you couldn't on this date."

A: "Boyfriends get to have sex with their girlfriends."

M: "No."

A: "It's beautiful. I'll give you so much pleasure."

Mila closes her eyes.

M: "Will you still respect me tomorrow?"

A: "No."

M: "Bad boyfriend."

A: "Okay, then, yes, I'll respect you in the morning."

M: "All right. I'm still a good girl. You may have me. It's my first time. Be gentle."

chapter 5

lovely utterances

Sunday, May 25, 2014
10:00 p.m.

From The White Sky: Andrés and Mila celebrate the carnal as soon as he arrives at her studio. The slow carnal. She runs it. Andrés comes to understand what it means to surrender to Mila's tactile sensibility – physical joy as never known from a woman's touch.

Clearly, she intends to give a massage.

A squeeze bottle of oil in one hand, Mila watches him remove the last of his clothing. She directs him to lay face down on the sturdy workbench table topped with a pad covered with time-softened sheets.

A: "What about these sheets?"

M: "These are old ones. Everything will wash out, so don't worry."

Mila lets her affection flow onto Andrés. In knowing him by touch, the hand of the sculptor brings soothing, conveys caring, summons eros – all three. They need no words. The only sounds ... the crack of logs in the fire, lovely utterances of release, and the faint slushing of skin on skin slicked with viscid oil.

M: "Turn over."

As he settles onto his back, the connection of eyes resumes. Mila multiplies the pleasure of sight by crossing her arms, tugging up her tank top, dropping off her other garments.

M: "There."

She makes a show of arching her back, displaying her naked torso. Then she resumes touching.

Several times her hands arrive right at the nexus of the man, her attentions making the organ shine and elongate.

Seemingly by silent understanding, the full erection does not yet appear. Her hands move on.

Even more intimate, Mila's fingers arrive at his face. Here they take on highest sensitivity, stroking, smoothing. She finds purchase under his cheekbones with the very tips of fingers, pulling there, then circling out around the eye sockets, down and back, finding his ears and squishing the softness of them under oil.

During this, his eyes open. She looks right in, not stopping her touch. The looping of connection deepens them, making warmth spread generously.

Descending his abdomen again, everything slows. Intention shifts. The consent of both contributes to the uplift of arousal. He becomes hard the moment her hand wraps around the shaft, and with two or three slow spiraling pulls, brings it to maximum heft.

The other hand grasps the oil bottle and spurts onto the erection an excess, a deliberate overwhelm of oil. Resistance to her stroking goes to zero. Mila can easily take things to the finish with determined strokes. Instead, she slows to a stop.

M: "Andrés."

He opens his eyes.

M: "Watch."

Mila does not remove her left hand from his cock. The right holds the oil bottle just below her neck and from it splashes the remainder of its contents across her chest. The quantity is excessive. She drops the bottle and splays her hand there. While sparks leap between in their glances, her hand spreads the oil across her torso, lifting and slicking her breasts, reaching up to circle her neck, swooping down again to make the oil cover her belly.

A: "Fucking beautiful."

Without detaching her eyes from his, she bends her left knee and lifts her foot onto the edge of the table. With all deliberate sensuality, her hand moves between the open thighs, finds the lips and eases them apart. Shiny fingers sink in, penetrating with a luscious sucking sound. Her other hand resumes stroking his cock.

Mila possesses sex and sex in hand and hand.

Hot and ready, she climbs onto the table, one foot on either side of his hips. Then, the lowering, the dropping, the touch of sex lips slid into position by her hand, kissing the head as if an open mouth, offered for the taking.

Mila closes her eyes, releases her weight. The cock eases in, pushing the interior walls apart. She shifts to set the flesh of her insides around it and squeezes.

A: "Fuck."

M: "Yes."

A: "Fuck."

Her hips begin to dance, face shameless and ambitious in pleasure. Both hands push oil around her belly, sliding to grasp and squish her breasts, letting the strong nipples slide between fingers.

A: "Fuck me."

Then a cadence on each snap of her pelvis.

A: "Fuck me. Fuck me. Fuck me."

Mila must hear his command, but her angle, her motions, her intent, focus on her own inflamed organs, especially the swollen clitoris both outside and inside, putting one hand there with smart fingers that increase the excitement: stroking, pulling, rubbing.

With increasing speed and power, with cries filling the studio, Mila rides to the top. Oil streams off everywhere. As if no excess of liquid were enough, both explode into the vortex, flooding with many juices, everything sloshed and slick with them, the tide of sex.

chapter 6

could heal the emptiness

Monday, May 26, 2014
12:20 a.m.

From The White Sky: They wake. There is a discussion about her art, her methods. They make a change to their consent agreement. Andrés thinks they are about to go back to sleep. She whispers one word in his ear ... he erupts ...

Andrés spins wildly and snatches Mila up with one arm around her waist. She squeals with excitement. He carries her to the table, still covered by the pad and oil-stained sheets, forces her torso face-down across it, legs dangling helplessly to the floor. She is bent at a ninety-degree angle. His knees force legs apart. With arrogant command, he penetrates in one swift stroke.

M: "No no no no no."

A: "Grab the edge of the table. You're like pudding inside. Squeeze hard. Tight."

She obeys with an earthy laugh. He tests with three massive strokes.

A: "Tighter."

Two more thrusts, right to the hilt.

M: "No no no. No. Stop."

His thrusting accelerates, consumed by the rage to penetrate.

Andrés twists her hair around his left hand and pulls her head back, the right hand encircling her exposed neck in a dangerous collaring. The weight of his hips pinning her down, his hard thing like a spike nailing her to the table, his hands immobilizing her head – this is his dark control.

He surges through her spluttering screams and pleadings with one hundred strokes. She grunts or blusters on each. The raw possession of femme builds furious lust in his pelvis. His hand on her throat feels every scream.

M: "Let go my hair."

A: "No."

He wants his juice in. Deep in. Splashing against the cervix. His last thrusts grow enormous, violent, to force her open fully. It requires ten spasms to release all. His voice roars into the room, bellowing on each ejaculation.

He collapses on her body. The deep void looms instantly – sadness and elation, so rich in the soul, yet still a void. If he stays in the woman, if his erection swells forever, maybe it could heal the emptiness.

A flash in the sullen quiet.

I could turn her over. Hold her eyes with mine. Forbid her to look away. Penetrate the hidden erotic refuge without asking, the fantastical one, the one poets say lies secreted in the breast of a woman, waiting for the man to breech it.

Prone on top of Mila, his breathing gradually slowing, he cherishes this dream, yet knows she will not allow it yet, will not allow his lovemaking to enter through the eyes to fully open her heart.

hilarious, cool, and challenging

Monday, May 26, 2014
1:30 a.m.

From The White Sky: After a walk on the night beach, Andrés and Mila return to the studio, the locus of their extreme affair, where every object vibrates because they make art, they make love, in this room. They engage in a no-limits exploration of their sexual daring, with extremes neither had approached with partners, ever.

Special advisory: this chapter is extreme in its conception and their daring.

A: "Okay, let's talk about sex. I'll tell you how it feels to take possession of your body like I just did. To control you and fuck you."

M: "Oh."

She shudders.

A: "Right there, that's a sex thing we have to discuss. You cringed."

M: "What?"

A: "That word. It's a wedge. People use it one of two ways, either to kick up the erotic, or to slash."

M: "Mostly negative. Fuck you!"

A: "That's right. To hurt the other person."

M: "When you said it just now, I felt the negative."

A: "Yeah, I saw it on your face, Mila. 'Fuck' was hurtful. I tried to say it as a turn-on, but it made you cringe."

M: "Yes. Even though we agreed to using it for the

good, right from our first time, it doesn't feel good. It feels crude and hurtful. Andrés, now that I think about it, the word 'fuck' is used like a weapon all the time. Everywhere."

A: "When actually it's about the life force. And if you're lucky, about romantic love."

M: "Oh my God. It's perverted!"

A: "'Fuck' has been perverted."

Their laughter tries to blow away the pain, but each sees distress on the face of the other.

M: "Sick."

A: "Yes. During a fight, if they aren't winning, people use it to do damage, even though it stands for –"

M: "For all that's holy. They use the holy thing to hurt."

Andrés is stopped by her words and the mischief on her face.

M: "What's the matter, Andrés, don't you know I'm a good Orthodox Catholic girl? A girl who secretly thinks sex is holy, like praying?"

A: "Whoa."

M: "Change the subject. Go back to 'fuck'."

Andrés is frozen by a thought. Mila sees, and waits.

A: "People sometimes use fucking – actual fucking – as a weapon."

Mila covers her mouth with her hand. Her eyes expand as she understands.

A: "Rape."

M: "Yes. It might as well be thought as rape. Angry fucking to put a hurt on the other."

They both allow the implications to reverberate. Nausea again.

M: "What are we going to do?"

A: "Can you think of another word that carries the power?"

M: "Screw?"

A: "Hurry home darling, I really want to screw you?"

M: "Guess not."

Andrés takes a moment to compose his thought.

A: "You felt 'fuck' as vulgar and obscene?"

M: "Yes. Even when I use it, there's a feeling of aggression on it. Sorry. We might have to stop saying it."

A: "I don't like it when people make it too common, either. Too unimportant."

M: "You mean, 'whatever?' Like, 'What the fuck'?"

A: "Yes, like that."

M: "Fuck is hurtful, or it means 'whatever?'"

A: "Yes. We have to do something about using the word in our bed. I wish I could say it would contribute to doing something about rape."

M: "If we straighten it out, if we make 'fuck' beautiful and sweet, we could achieve world peace."

They should have laughed. It is a perfect jape by Mila. They do not laugh. In one corner of his unlaughing reaction, Andrés glimpses the ugly truth: this is no joke.

A: "Most people would think this conversation is pitiful. Intellectuals talking about sex instead of doing it."

M: "This is our bespoke night to talk it out. Then we won't have to for a while. Keep going."

A: "Bespoke? I've never heard that word. I'll look up later, okay? But I get it. Okay, forget about 'fuck,' we can't solve that problem right now. So, let's keep going. You wanted to talk about sex, go ahead."

M: "That time, when I gave you my safe word and you crashed onto me over the table, you made me orgasm with your wicked mouth, and then lifted me off the floor and carried me into bed, and I began to resist?"

M: "Yes?"

M: "You made me put my fingers in. You ordered me to put my fingers in deep. There was a split second when I was resisting, bam, then you were forcing me against my will, bam, then I let go, bam. One-two-three, bam-bam-bam."

A: "Your insides turned wet."

M: "What?"

A: "Turned wet. The exact second you let go of the resistance. An instant flood inside. I felt it."

M: "Yes. Resisting, then surrendering, it gets me excited. I like it more than orgasm."

A: "No, you don't."

M: "Oh yes. Seeing you come at me, holding out, you keep tugging at me, trying to spread me open, fighting you, and then I give up. I let you. That is so fucking hot."

A: "I would do anything to get in."

M: "Get in?"

A: "In cunt."

She moves closer. Her eyes narrow to slits, pulling inward to darkness.

M: "I love that word. I love it so. It's beautiful-dirty. You've never said it so far."

A: "No. I wanted to wait until I got to know you better."

Mila screams with laughter. Their eyes dance. Then she turns serious.

M: "Okay, Andrés Quevara, now we have to clean up *that* word?"

A: "Yes."

M: "Talk about a word that means something beautiful, but it gets used as a weapon. Oh my God, it's perverted!"

A: "What is perverted?"

Mila hesitates. She is not shy, not embarrassed. Something else.

M: "Wait. Only you say it."

A: "What?"

M: "I'm making up a thing, right now. Here's the thing: I don't want to say it. I didn't lie, Andrés, I actually love that word. But only you say it."

A: "It doesn't pull in the negative? The hate and shame?"

M: "No. I think I know why."

A: "Why?"

M: "I'm not going to say this word, Andrés. Not going to say it 'in our bed,' and I promise I won't use it as a weapon when we fight. I'm holding out on saying it. Until ... I can't hold out. Okay? You say it. Don't say it too often, but I love you saying it. Don't say it too often, save it. Then hit me with it. And don't ever say those other words for it. I hate almost every other word for it except 'vagina.' That's why it doesn't pull in the negative when you say it."

A: "Really."

M: "Yes. When I hear it out in the culture used to sting – to humiliate and shame – I get really angry, but the word itself is not damaged in me. It's mine, and I want you to use that word, the 'c' word, just at the right time. Not too often. By the way, this word was applied man to man in rude society in England – not to women. At first."

His grownup cute girlfriend is an intellectual on sex. Hilarious, cool, and challenging. He pauses. Then he whispers right into her eager face.

A: "I love your cunt."

Her eyes close and a shudder racks her body. He lets it reach bottom and rise back up her torso until it makes her eyes tear up when she opens them.

M: "Please, Andrés, say it one more time. But only once. Hurt me with it. So good."

A: "Look in my eyes. There. Like that. I've had my cock in your mouth tonight."

M: "Yes. Put it in again."

A: "No. Not yet. Agree to something."

M: "What?"

A: "When I put it in, you have to imagine that it is not your mouth."

M: "What?"

A: "Imagine your mouth is your sex."

Her eyes close again.

A: "No! Look at me."

Her eyes snap open. She dare not look away. Her breathing races to catch up to the thrill of his erotic imagination setting itself on her.

M: "Your mouth. Right now. Right now, let it be."

He watches his order sink into her visage. She is shaking.

He takes his eyes off hers, focuses right on her red lips,
right where he knew she was feeling everything.

A: "Is it?"

She nods.

A: "Open it like you do when I tell you to spread open
the lips between your legs. Just a little."

She separates the lips and opens her mouth, revealing
pink wet insides.

A: "It's so sweet. Let the wetness build up in there.
Don't swallow. I'm going to fuck it."

Mila shudders.

A: "You know I'm going to fuck it, right now."

M: "Yes."

A: "We're taking the ugly out of the word 'fuck,' Mila."

M: "Yes."

A: "I'm going to fuck you now."

M: "Oh my God."

A: "You say that a lot. 'Oh my God.' You say it in our
bed."

M: "Yes."

A: "Well 'in our bed' just became a thing for us. It
means all our sex, all our eroticism."

M: "Yes. 'In our bed' means all our sex and erotic play."

A: "Don't take your eyes from mine. There. Now just a
little, let it open, there, a little, more. Not too open.
Perfect."

Andrés calms his center. Her brave eyes hold steady.

A: "I'm going to put my cock right there, right at the
opening. I'll be slow and careful. Relax and let me,
because I am going to sink all the way in. All the way to
the bottom of your cunt."

Her eyes well up with tears of burning, burning with
lust for his sexual heart, which loves to bruise and cherish
hers.

A: "I'll come out right away, but then thrust in again, a
little faster. I'll stay in longer, too. Then two more times.
I'm going to fuck you deep. Four times."

The consent comes from a tiny nod. He looks inside

again. It is pink, delicate and surrendered. Then with power and confidence he swirls above, in place on the sofa. Her head adjusts to the angle. He places the tip right there. Her lips form softly in a circle around. It is beautiful to see, looking down.

Her eyes close. Mila will still not let him look in her eyes on penetration.

A: "Don't swallow anything."

Then, in one easy press of weight and authority, he eases his organ into her mouth, stopping at the beginning of her throat. Finding willingness, surrender, invitation, he carefully eases past the flesh at the back. He is in.

Then out – delicious with her soft lips dragging on him, letting the rim bump. The next thrust, perfectly smooth until almost all the way, yet pausing slightly to be sure to not choke, then pressing home when he is sure it would not. A long groan comes from the throat as he pulls out.

The third slides in splendidly. All the way in, with a slushing sound made from compression of flowing juices. Then back.

The last. Andrés loses all context. He is only the thrusting, pushing, urging force. Even as the stroke penetrates fully, stays buried, he understands nothing but the white-hot drive to fuck. He wants to slam his cock down her throat for hours.

But he pulls out. Collapses onto the sofa.

The sight of Mila's face shocks. Everything is wet and flushed. The flesh flames red, the tissues of lips and cheeks swollen. So much saliva flows, her lips and chin shine bright with it and tendrils trail onto her breasts. She makes no move to hide or wipe anything away. Eyes, heavy eyes, do not blink. She is still surrendered, still holding the illusion.

A: "Let go now. Let it be your mouth again."

She cannot speak at first. They just breathe into it together. She is so beautiful. Gradually, her composure returns. He takes a towel and holds it to her face. Tenderness in caring.

M: "Oh Andrés..."
A: "That's how much I want your cunt, all the time."
M: "Oh."

The scared and wonderful thrill on her face affects Andrés. He will never forget how she looks in this moment. A woman has allowed him to unleash the male primitive, and still she does not run, does not mask her concupiscence, does not withdraw her consent. She is proud. Proud of her share of the carnal in bed with him.

Eventually she smiles shyly. He remains very close, kissing her mouth. That is hot, those kisses on the mouth, now. They say nothing for many minutes, holding each other, loving the quiet in the studio with bright stars and a quarter moon shining through the skylights.

Then, for another hour, they talk about sex. They disarm the two radioactive words. They do this by saying them both over and over with no aggression in them, no shame in them, only respect and affection.

Eventually, they celebrate the victory of having won back the powerful words by sharing sweet orgasms during intercourse.

This achieves world peace.

the root of her person

Monday, May 26, 2014
3:45 a.m.

From The White Sky: Andrés feels the insides of the new boundaries and freedoms they have established in the night ...

Andrés takes possession by tenderness.

A: "Turn around."

She spins in place. From behind his arms circle her torso. He unbuttons the first two buttons of her shirt with forearms and sides of hands pressing her breasts, an indirect caress of sexual charm.

A: "Don't move."

His mouth at the side of her neck leaves wicked kisses. Sensing the nearly imperceptible hairs there, how lightly can he kiss? He skims above the flesh. He can sense the bend and release of ethereal strands.

The press of his body from behind grows slight, mere suggestion. Mila's breathing quickens. He matches her exhales with his, sends them over the shoulder down the front to ruffle the edge of the blouse. This raises gooseflesh. Then, to direct breaths under her chin, back behind her ear, down her arm. One hand pulls aside the edge of the garment to expose the side of a breast. He aims his breath there. She shudders.

A: "Bring both hands up behind your neck. Under your hair. Now pull it up, pile it on top. Point your elbows up. High."

When Mila obeys, it exposes the back of her neck, rich with downy hairs. These receive his zephyr breaths, the faint press of lips, the tip of tongue barely grazing. How

beautiful it looks, the arc of her hairline, exposed now, a
private curve seldom revealed. There is a forward cant to
her neck, that coy bend yet with upright posture, as if a
bow of humility to the beauty of this secret place. Andrés
brings the adoring kisses, the tiny ones, the maddeningly
sweet tenderness, his breath inflaming with coolness
when he lifts off to move his mouth to the next spot. She
breathes faster with each, desperate for enough oxygen to
suffer pleasure.

Then he shifts intent. His mouth opens and takes the
back of her neck in a wide, wet kiss. The sudden lewdness
wrenches a pitiful groan from Mila. He slides his mouth,
leaving a wet trail along the hairline. She shakes under the
press of his lips and release of too much wetness. He does
not relent for four such kisses.

Then he pulls his mouth away.

M: "Andrés ..."

A: "Quiet. I'm binding your arms now. They are bound
together. I'm hanging them tight from a rope tied to the
skylight. You can't lower them. Make sure your hands
hold your hair up like this."

M: "Yes, Andrés."

A: "Now I'm blindfolding you. Close your eyes."

M: "Yes."

A: "Don't speak."

He withdraws all contact. Mila is left to hang
suspended, his touch suspended, time suspended – to
make her swell with hunger. With her eyes shut and her
back turned, in the absence of touch, Mila twists with
nerves on edge from the subtle torture. Andrés holds the
tableau for long minutes, making her agonize in silence.
Then he feeds a provocative sound – that of his clothes
falling from his body. He makes sure, especially, to jangle
the buckle of his belt when unfastened. He finishes the
maneuver by kicking the clothing aside, clearly audible
across the floor in the night.

Then silence returns. She hangs suspended, blinded.
Still he does not hurry. He approaches from behind with

slow steps. She twists when his heat and breath caress her. Then another silent minute with him standing right behind.

There has been no touching, no words, for fully ten minutes.

His hands hover at her sides. The half-unbuttoned blouse, pulled up by her raised arms, fails to cover at the waist. With utter gentleness, he lays both hands on her sides just above the jut of hipbones. She writhes.

M: "Ohhh."

He does not admonish her for crying out, savoring the failure of her obedience. Always, to make a woman cry out, so exciting.

A transit of hands up under the shirt begins, so light, so slow. Mila moans and shakes under his hands.

A: "Don't move."

Her breasts fill his hands. He lifts them, weighs them, cherishes them. Nipples slip through fingers. He is taking his woman and her breasts in his hands. In his throat and belly the sumptuous savor of control overflows.

Andrés slips around to come in front of her bound body. He releases the remaining buttons of her shirt. The right hand, in front, rises to her neck and grasps it around. Its forearm maintains intimate pressing on soft breasts. The other goes up her back, under the blouse, its forearm lifting it. Andrés touches her back gently, everywhere.

A: "See? Now it's my turn to know your torso under your shirt."

His left hand slips across her shoulders into a sleeve. In a rapid motion, he yanks the shirt high, pulls it firmly back, and twists it tight so it forms a binding across the shoulders and upper arms. Her elbows remain pointed up, her hands in her hair.

M: "No, no. Oh no."

A: "Quiet. I'm binding you."

His hand entwined in the shirt asserts harsh control. He uses leverage to sway her body, rotate it, bend it back to expose undefended targets for his mouth, which descends on breasts and takes nipples of each one at a time inside.

She moans his name, hissing out the sibilant.

M: "Andréssss..."

He drinks them. Sucks them. Pulls the hard buds into erection. She wiggles against the constraints, only making his force grow. He insinuates one thigh between hers, his cock smashing against her naked abdomen. With the new angle, the bending back of her waist, the free hand now at the base of her spine pulls her forward, demands surrender of her core. Andrés takes full possession in this moment.

His mouth comes up to hers, opens it rudely. His lips, teeth, tongue, the flesh of his face go in her mouth. He senses shocked rigidity. This he attacks with sensual insistence, wet insistence. *Yes, I am invading you. Let me.* She cannot hold out – her mouth melts from lips all the way to the back of her throat.

Andrés roams inside. He slicks across teeth, he inhales her tongue, he pours saliva forth, mixing his with hers, filling the space between. It is lewd, extreme, and breathtakingly erotic. Not a kiss – a liquid devour. Only whimpers escape her throat, and they vibrate in the wet.

He pulls his mouth off.

A: "You are still blindfolded. I'm cutting the rope from the ceiling."

Using the shirt twisted around her shoulders and his grip at her waist, he pulls her to the bed, moving fast, half dragging her, making sure her stumbling efforts to keep up do not stop forward progress. He picks her up with the other arm and drops her face-up, dead center on the mattress.

A: "Spread your legs."

She does it too slowly. Keeping his left hand in control of her head with the shirt-binding, he uses the right to push her legs wide, roughly. Slipping the free hand around her hip, he grasps one cheek, pulls it wide from the other, gets one finger locked under a lip so the mouth between her legs splits wide open.

Then, with the speed of a primordial cat, Andrés mounts into place, thrusts in. He is in Mila again. That is all.

In.

The surrender of the woman below, the yielding, the letting … the exquisite letting … she is surely his for the possessing.

His sexual heart blossoms free, strong, and bold. Nothing blocks his power in this high place. He has won. His strokes depart from all concern, all but dropping deep to find nothing stopping him at the root of her person, finding the way up through the delicious soaking cunt full of spasms, then rocketing above, reaching the white void into which he flings his wild juice, there, there, and there.

chapter 9

all female grace

Monday, May 26, 2014
11:20 p.m.

From The White Sky: Mila doubts. Unreality sweeps over her self-opinions. Does he really want me for sex? Andrés is delighted to respond.

"You are going to have to get used to the fact that at least one man on this island gets turned on by a woman, not a girl."

Mila's eyes close.

"I still don't believe it. I believe it, but I don't believe it."

"I'm not trying to tell you I'm in love with you. But you can take my ridiculously engorged organ's word for it – I am in lust for you."

Mila emits a blubbering laugh.

A: "Keep looking in my eyes. Keep stroking. Not fast."
She faces him, kneeling at his left side as he sits, hand on his trousers sliding along his erection.
A: "Get me naked now."
Milla strips him bare, he sinks deep into the couch, she sits adjacent, left hand on his organ.
A: "Did you like that word 'engorged?'"
She laughs and nods her head.
A: "I said it to be ridiculous. How long do you think it could stay ... engorged?"
M: "Half an hour?"
A: "Two hours."
M: "What?"

A: "I want you to see it staying hard for two hours, engorged and wanting to fuck you."

The word jolts her. Wakes her. Her eyes glint and her hand slows its action.

A: "After two hours of having it in your hand and in your mouth, it'll still be hard. Then I'm going to make you admit how much I want to fuck you. Anytime Mila is in the vicinity, I want to fuck her. Say it."

M: "Anytime Mila is in the vicinity, Andrés wants to fuck her."

A: "Immediately, every time, right away. Sometimes I don't do anything about it, but I still want to."

M: "I'm just moving around, just ordinary life, and if you see me you want to fuck me?"

A: "Yes."

M: "Even if I'm in a real bitchy mood?"

A: "Yes. I'm going to stay hard for two hours, make you come with my fingers or my mouth. You'll be coming, I'll be hard. Say it again."

M: "Anytime Andrés is around Mila, he wants to fuck her."

A: "Take it in your mouth now. Show me how sweetly you can do it. Sweetest ever."

Her eyes hold his for one last second. As she turns away, her mouth opens. A glimpse of the pink inside jerks up the erotic. Then Mila, obeying, brings gentle softness. She slithers the head in, holds it in suspension with such light pressure he believes her mouth has quit working. But then lips press again. She draws her mouth back, letting the rim bump on its way out.

Twice more. No increase of speed, no lessening of tenderness.

Andrés leans forward on the chair and draws her face up to his. They make tender kisses. She enwraps his tongue with her lips, the same lips that just cradled his cock. He is sharply aware of that. Her left hand wraps around the shaft, during.

A: "So sweet."

M: "So sweet."

A: "Your mouth tender on my cock makes it hard."

M: "I like my mouth tender on it, even way deep in my mouth."

A: "Try that."

Mila takes his organ with even slower sensuality. Just the head and first inch. Her tongue laves from under. She pauses with not even a rocking motion, a perfect beat of sexual drama. Then, she uses all female grace to ease him in deep, the tip penetrating to the beginning of her throat, and with a final surrender takes it past, down, in.

A: "Oh. Oh."

Mila holds, relaxes, senses the engulfment, then slips him out.

A: "And your mouth kisses mine tender even when it's all the way in mine. How do you know to kiss like that, Mila?"

M: "I know how to kiss deep in you and tender because you fuck me hard. You slam me hard, so I kiss tender."

A: "Try that."

M: "We are so damn oral, Andrés. Going for the world record."

A: "We are so oral. It would be a deal killer, all this talking, except for two things."

M: "Talk to me. Don't stop talking. Make me take your cock down my throat, but first keep talking. What are the two things?"

Andrés laughed. Once again – he has met his match.

A: "First, we don't just talk. Second, we are both oral."

M: "Yes. I hope there's enough oxygen in the world."

A: "But kissing you roughly, controlling your mouth with mine. Do you like that way of kissing too?"

M: "Yes. Lewd kissing, sometimes."

A: "Why do you like it?"

M: "Your juices mix with mine."

A: "Like it's way too much juice, so rude, but then not."

M: "Yes."

A: "Next kiss more. There will be even more wetness."

M: "Yes, Andrés."

A: "I'm going to lick you deep in your throat."

Her breathing speeds up. She looks right in his eyes.

A: "You must go totally relaxed. My hand will be around your throat. I want the taste of the inside of your mouth in mine. Eat you and drink you. Extreme."

M: "Fill my mouth. Then drink it."

A: "You won't swallow?"

M: "I won't."

A: "You think I'm going to do it now."

M: "Please lick me deep inside here." She strokes her throat with her expressive left hand.

A: "No. Get on the bed. Face up."

She leaps up and runs to throw herself on it.

Andrés slows when he gets to the edge of the bed. An existential hot spot catches up with him – girl in bed.

A: "Fuck, just the sight of naked-girl Mila in a bed makes it hard!"

Mila laughs. She starts to touch herself.

A: "No!"

She jerks her hands away.

A: "Just watch and listen."

He takes his organ in hand. Stroking, he goes into a stream...

A: "girl in sheets. naked. unprotected. naked. the vee, it will fall open. get it open. lips open. she forgets her breasts. they beg me, she does not know. when she pulls a shirt off. gets naked, runs jumps in bed. infuriating. makes my eyes water. roll over. girl bottom rounding up. fit there, naked. no, not yet. a naked girl in my bed ... so cool."

He strokes away to this litany, standing over her, his blinding erotic drives reaching the surface. The short path to exploding appears. One, two more strokes. He slows.

A: "I'd love to get you in bed, make you roll around in the sheets and open your legs, make you put fingers in, then just blast off over and over and put it all over you. Ten times. Full blasts all over your body. If I had as much juice as girls do, I'd just keep spraying it on your body and face. I. Would. Just. Love. That."

M: "I would take every splash."

A: "That extreme kiss is coming."

M: "I'm ready."

A: "But I want the taste of your other mouth in my mouth first."

M: "Oh."

He loves making her make that sound. Make Mila say 'oh.'

A: "Do what I tell you, but slow … keep your legs together, but bend at the waist and pull them as far up and back as you can. Use your hands to pull them up."

The naked girl in the bed performs this ballet very well. Legs straight, fully folded at the waist, she can almost make her toes touch the sheet above her head. Bent-in-two girl. The hands behind her thighs hold the legs together and pull them over her left shoulder. She keeps swaying them back and forth a few inches and he imagines the effect between, the lips at her vortex rubbing against one another.

He sits on the edge of the bed. Mila stares at his cock jutting up.

A: "Listen carefully. This is about you offering. Not about you letting. Not about me taking. It's about you offering. Period."

M: "How do I do that?"

A: "You can help me annihilate something from my sexual history. I call them the 'no-big-deal' girls."

Mila gives a quick laugh to that. She sways her legs and hips seductively.

M: "What the hell is that?"

A: "A man wants the woman to let him in, but usually she's too easy about it, with no importance attached to it. Like it's nothing special. Wham, they spread open in a flash and the offering of their sexual self means nothing."

M: "Oh."

A: "Do you like holding your legs tight together, but

bent back like that? Over your shoulder?"

M: "Yes."

She pulls them and sways them more, like a semaphore of sex to come.

A: "We're going to destroy the too-easiness."

M: "How can I make it mean something to you?"

A: "No, not to me. Make it mean something to you."

M: "Oh."

A: "Between is your sex."

M: "Yes."

A: "You're going to let me in. But don't just give it. Make me deserve it. Feel the privacy of it hidden between right now."

She closes her eyes. Her bottom swivels slightly and she squeezes the legs together more.

M: "Do you mind being my teacher? I should know all this already and be your perfect mistress. I'm a grown woman, not a witless virgin."

A: "Shussssh."

M: "Okay."

A: "That's why you press your legs together, to protect the privacy."

M: "Yes."

M: "I want you to hold your legs a certain way. A certain way. Keep them closed and put privacy in between. Hide your body in a pool of modesty. Deep in."

A: "Okay."

He watches the effect in her visage. Mila goes chaste. He sees she is really doing it, really becoming innocent.

A: "When you're ready, part them. You can keep your hands behind your knees to get there. Keep the modesty, but add surrender and exposure. Think of all your female privacy and girly goodness, but then open your legs with lust in your heart. Like a wanton girl."

Her eyes close and a deep breath fills her chest.

A: "All men want it. Keep it from them. Be proud how important it is, how sacred. Worshipful. Don't let them, make them wait, don't let them.

M: "They can't have it."

A: "Right. But with no man around ... in secret, with no one watching, spread wide open and offer it."

M: "Just offering?"

A: "Exactly. Offer to the universe."

She shifts her bottom to slip even deeper into the bed. To angle the pelvis, he knows. One hand behind each knee, legs point straight up.

A: "Bend the knees. There. Do you feel the privacy and modesty between your legs?"

Her eyes close. He sees her unashamedness change to protectiveness. That's what he wants. Mila nods.

A: "The too-easy world has forgotten the existence of anything private and modest. If anyone brings it up, they mock it. Sneer at it."

M: "I can channel the good Catholic girl."

A: "Okay, but no guilt or shame with it. Only genuine, healthy modesty. But then add sex-heat when you open your legs. It's not you letting me take it. It's you offering it ... to the universe. Just for the pure sake of offering. Close your eyes and forget about me – I am not here, no one is. Now, use your hands and thigh muscles and move everything until you find the most exposed place. Where it is offered, unconditionally, unprotected, naked."

Mila understands. Her eyes close and she feels her way. She eases the thighs apart. She closes them again and pulls her knees up to her chest. Then she eases back. The knees come down and spread. Her breathing speeds up as she pulls her legs around, seeking the sweet spot.

Then, she finds it. Legs angle apart at just under ninety-degrees. Between thighs – Mila's vulnerability. Mila's exposure.

M: "Oh. I didn't know."

A: "Keep holding like that. Mila, this is for you. Not for me. You are offering it and all the sex in you. It's your cunt."

Mila quivers and her eyes close.

"The whole. Everything that is you and your sex. It's all

the goodness and beauty in your cunt."

Her breathing races. She is transfixed by that word.

M: "I want to take my hands away. May I?"

A: "Yes."

She lowers her hands to the bed. Her legs sway, part more, return to position. She can find the place as if by radar now.

M: "It feels so good in my chest and belly. It's innocent and private, but erotic too."

A: "Would you do it when you're alone sometimes?"

M: "Oh my God, yes. Wait, Andrés, let me close my legs and start over."

A: "Yes."

She closes her thighs and drops her legs flat on the bed. Likewise, her hands – they will not engage this time. Straight at the knees, she raises her legs high, thighs together, toes pointing to the skylights. Hold. Then, all in one slow motion, the knees bend, the angle at the waist drops, and thighs part. Obediently, her focus is inward – on herself – seeking the locus of female secret sex to offer.

M: "There."

The swaying and lifting comes to a stop.

M: "There. There it is. There."

Andrés moves between. He senses no protection.

A: "I just arrived in this palace. I find you beautiful and exposed. It is yours. May I have it?"

M: "Yes. Oh yes oh yes oh yes."

He takes the offered yoni in his mouth.

M: "Oh oh oh oh oh."

The shock of pleasure does not cause her to pull back or freeze. No, with a sensuous sway, the sex of this bold woman slips forward to him.

He revels in all senses: the slithering softness against his lips, the gorgeous taste and scent like essence of the sea, the slushing noises of her liquids splashing against those in his mouth, and the pinks and reds of blood-filled lips and folds, exquisitely pulsing before his eyes.

He does not hurry. He loves the sounds she makes as his

mouth shifts, finding new flesh, provoking the inside and outside of the clit into erection, reaching in far with his tongue. Mila never abandons the offered position. Strong thighs keep her legs aloft, spread and steady, even with no support from her hands. The hands lie softly on the bed.

M: "... wide open. So fucking wide open. And sweet and innocent."

Andrés uses his lips to expose her sex more than ever, and thrusts his mouth in. Her hips sway to his actions. She aims the opening best to let him.

M: "Sweet and innocent. And so fucking dirty-beautiful. Eat me."

He drinks her, sucks her, licks the opened organs with no restraint. Surrounding her seizures of pleasure and cries of joy, a new abandon envelops the bed: her limpid vulnerability. It does not require two hours to devour her doubts.

chapter 10

salacious

Tuesday, May 27, 2014
11:00 p.m.

From The White Sky: Very beautifully, on arrival in Vineyard Haven at her studio, Mila and Andrés walk hand-in-hand to the sleeping area, undress each other, lay on the bed, and with hardly a word, bring their bodies together for sex. It is tender and quick.

Mila moves on top. They have not kissed, have not caressed with hands.

M: "Foreplay with you already in me."

He gives a small nod. She takes his organ in hand. With a few strokes it achieves fine hardness. She eases the head into her parted lips and sinks down, shifting until fully impaled and hips comfortable. Then – something wonderful – she leans forward and down to rest her torso on his, straightens her legs so they rest on his, turns her head to rest on his chest and places both hands palm down to rest on his shoulders. Her petite pear-shaped frame rests on his body as if she were sunning on a raft in a lake.

Right up inside her sex, however, stands his.

Mila closes her eyes and sighs deeply. Andrés brings his hands to her back and caresses with soft touches. These evolve into fingertips only. He can reach all the way to her rounded backside, so her body from there up to the tip of her head comes under his attention. Fingertips only.

Mila takes the touching. She answers each caress with a squeeze of the muscles surrounding her vagina, a sexy call and response.

A: "Feels so good with you on me. A naked girl lying on me."

M: "You should always have a naked girl lying on you."

A: "So much skin on mine, with perfect weight pressing. Especially breasts pressing. They poke me to distraction."

She giggles and squeezes him tight below.

M: "I wish they were bigger."

A: "No."

Andrés sighs. He keeps his hands in motion, drifting up and down her body. Once he fits both hands onto her bottom and moves the flesh in circles, then pulls up. She matches with cooperative squeezing. Then his traversing of her back with fingertips resumes.

His hand comes up and fits under her hair, cupping the back of her neck.

A: "Inch up a little. I want to put my mouth in yours."

She slips one arm around his neck and pulls up with it. They stay joined below.

Then they are kissing. At first in no hurry, lips graze lips and gradually open to let wet graze wet inside. His hand at her neck rotates her head to fit them together with more and more insistence. She heats faster than he – her tongue slips into his mouth and goes exploring. With daring. Soon she is licking his insides as if a luscious ice cream cone melting too fast. This pulses his cock, quicker the more outrageous Mila's tongue inside his mouth goes wild.

Andrés releases his hand from the back of her neck. She does not slow her uninhibited kissing. Her head rotates to force more and more of her mouth inside his, twisting to slush around. She groans inside it all.

The continuously occurring kissing is the hallmark of their oral love affair. They cannot get enough kissing. They never get bored. They stay outrageous with their mouths, on purpose.

Mila rises up out of the kiss and sits straight up. Her pelvis rotates and her squeezing turns into strokes, strokes that slide up and back into and onto his cock.

A: "Like that. Like that, like that."

The miracle of Mila's quickening, her speed of ascent, amazes him once again. *How hot is this woman?* Just like that, her sleepy sunbath on a raft has turned into a new joyride, into endgame. He sees her hand go to the femme juncture, pulling and rubbing there. She cries out on each of her strokes. He begins to thrust back. Then her cries warp into moaning, deep from the gut. Once, twice, again, she slams a powerful stroke and down-squeeze. On the last she never rises. He feels the inside shuddering, sure that she is contracting all the way into her cervix.

M: "Oh oh oh. Fuck oh...."

The pleasure in her face is a thrill all its own. He holds still and hard while her after-climax endures. It is at least a minute of heavy breathing, glistening eyes, and soft sighing.

He flips her over and they un-join.

M: "Wait."

Her legs slowly rise. She uses hands beneath thighs to achieve the full bend. One arm wraps around under the back of knees, holds them together, pulls them up high. A hand caresses the puffy mound between the closed thighs. Three fingers disappear completely. They glisten when slipped out. She forces them in again. A salacious juicy sound accompanies every penetration.

M: "Put it in here. Put it in and come. Give me every drop all the way in. Spray me."

Andrés moves into place. As expected, her eyes close. Her fingers continue to stroke the soaked sex. He grabs her wrist and yanks her hand out, throwing it to the side, then replaces it with his fat cock and fucks hard and deep in, in, in.

Within twenty strokes, while she incites him with beggings of 'fuck me, fuck me, fuck me,' he empties large and fully into his wet girlfriend.

.

chapter 11

tender silk tapestry

Wednesday, May 28, 2014
8:10 p.m.

From The White Sky: Mila says, "Oh, you think you have confidence?"
Andrés: "All kinds of confidence. I'm qualified to be in charge of everything."
An electric current zaps them. Wattage increases for three sizzling seconds. Then she whispers:
"Time in."

A: "I'll show you how confident."

He strips naked. He does not care what she does, nor does he instruct. When nude, he starts a march toward the bed. As if picking up a sack of grain from the floor of a barn, he grabs Mila and throws her over his shoulder without losing stride. She adopts silent mode. A hot gambit – he knows she knows the silence turns him on. Not a sound. Like a sack of grain.

Spilling her onto the bed, he yanks off her studio shoes, pulls off her socks and reaches for the zipper at the front of her jeans. Mila stares up at him, reactionless. Andrés continues stripping her bare.

M: "I always come first."

A: "Did you say something?"

He yanks the shirt up over her head. He has a girl naked in bed. His urgency accelerates, hands push legs apart, fit themselves behind knees, and in one motion bends her fully at the waist, urging the knees up to her chest. Full of audacity like the untamed gaucho of her imagination, he penetrates in one thrust all the way deep.

She lets out an involuntary grunt.

A: "Quiet. Your mouth is bound. You can't speak."

He does not look in her face. He does not check her state of arousal – it is none of his business. Andrés is on trajectory, already approaching escape velocity. He arrives with thirty strokes, blatantly un-tinged with doubt, bellowing victory, shuddering wildly, slamming his juice home with power into the silent woman. He pulls out, flips over onto his back, cradling his organ with his hand, polishing the aftershocks into full pleasure with no inhibition.

The body he used lies quietly on the bed. His heaving downslope savors that. No visitors. After enjoying for what would have been the length of a cigarette, he sits up, not looking at her. She has not moved. He eventually speaks ...

A: "I have another one."

M: "Can I have it?"

A: "I'm going to empty into you again, in about half-an-hour."

M: "You are using me."

A: "Yes."

M: "I want it sooner."

Andrés takes seven seconds to think. Not a long time, but her panic blossoms in it – she is not allowed to speak. She spoke. What if he never answers.

A: "You can try provoking me with sounds between your legs. Use your fingers. Let me hear you pushing the wetness around. That might get me to penetrate you sooner."

He moves to a chair next to the bed. He reaches across and turns off a lamp on a side table and the studio is plunged into darkness.

He hears evidence his orders are being obeyed. Mila's breathing is audible and deepening. She issues little cooing sounds. And the lusciousness of something wet – provoked, stirred, sloshed.

He waits in the dark fully ten minutes, slowly stroking his cock. She achieves orgasm during. He hears it as if the sound of lovers in the next room. Even though just expended, his organ stays hard, but the rage to thrust it into her has not caught up. The sound of pleasuring and thrashing in the bed continues, steadily, with no actual words from the girl's mouth. He smiles in the dark. She is so fucking obedient. A few muffled growls leak out, however, because she is touching herself to come again. His smile gets bigger with another thought. This is Mila, rebellious, obstinate, hardcore Mila, who has no business being obedient. He has turned her with his cock.

Then he whispers to incite.

A: "Come as many times as you want."

She groans.

M: "Andrés ..."

A: "Quiet."

He pauses for a second, then issues a reprimand.

A: "Only the sounds from between your legs. No words. And no moaning. I am binding your mouth with duct tape."

He reaches over and covers her mouth with his left hand. The restraint is tight and scary. Not to speak, not to utter a sound, not to release in that way. Her breathing bears the burden and her fingers speed up, seeking to reach explosion and thus escape his control. She is furious.

He lets it go on for minutes. Then he boils over.

Andrés leaps off the chair, launches onto the bed, grabs her by the waist to flip her over. He thrusts her legs apart and shoves his hand into the vortex, finding girl-fingers knuckle deep. He pulls her slippery hands away, gathers them together at the small of her back, squeezes them tight with his grip, mounts into position, and thrusts with all his weight deep into her from behind.

She screams into a pillow.

A: "Quiet! No sounds. I've bound your mouth."

His feet wedge into place against a cross-timber at the end of the bed. This gives leverage. It doubles the speed and solidity of his thrusting, with devastating effect on the helpless wet cunt below. The sound of his cock pounding into liquids might be that of some flood annihilating a muddy shore.

A: "You. Can. Only. Scream. When. You. Come."

She obeys. With every thrust he feels her throw the forbidden moan onto a bank of girl-lust – which will erupt when she gets there. He knows how to attack from behind to provoke her inside-clitoris. He aims there, puts it on repeat, then forgets her altogether.

The thrill in his chest is no longer confidence – his ecstatic libido leaves that notion far behind. It is triumph.

He hears the roar of Mila claiming pleasure. His orgasm rolls down his spine, explodes in his pelvis and spills out of his cock with one, two, three emphatic thrusts. He finishes with five slow, heavy, gratifying penetrations, each of which expels a drop, none of which encounter any resistance whatsoever. He has put them into the vast erotic void.

Collapsing onto the body below him, no longer striving, no longer conquering, he notices the tender silk tapestry of lovely Mila wrapped around his heart. He peels it off and drapes it over both their prone bodies, with affection, smiling.

It is stained with both their juices.

pitiful begging
Friday, May 30, 2014
6:50 p.m.

From The White Sky: was away for 48 hours. "Rain,"
she yells as he marches at her in the doorway of the
studio. She had heard him racing up the driveway.
"I'm waterproof." Then they crash together and
talking becomes impossible.

It is kissing that makes talking impossible.

Their oral paradox: sexy talking makes them kiss, so they cannot talk.

Instead, touching while kissing. Hands on someone, charged-up, sex-starved organs naked and exposed, you touch ... you melt, like syrup, like runoff of a succulent oil-bath unable to quench the aroused flesh.

Andrés wants his hands on her belly and breasts while kissing. He gets behind her. He twists half-sideways, tucks her shoulder under, gets his mouth on her neck and roams aggressively up until his head eases hers to the side so he can seal her mouth with his. Kissing from behind. Both his hands fit under her breasts.

Mila utters satisfaction sounds. She is ample in making them. He is addicted to the effect of her exclamations on his arousal, would kiss her wildly like this all day to hear them. Little sighs and giggles -- she cannot speak words due to his mouth clamped on hers.

Their oral paradox.

Without ending the kiss, her arms rise and arc over her shoulders, and his, grasping him behind the neck. This gives her leverage to pull her body into an S-curve, bottom wiggling and thrusting back into him, blatantly seeking to inflame everything by rolling on his organ.

Andrés keeps her from falling forward with firm control
of her upper body, hands full of her breasts. Only by his
height advantage and her flexibility can they keep their
mouths sealed. The kiss is savage, not sweet. Brazen.

She spins around, slashing free from his grip. They strip
each other bare – inefficiently due to wild kissing.

Then Andrés gets his hands under her bottom and
begins a lift. She pulls up with her arms around his neck,
folds her legs at knees and waist. He slides her up, until
her navel arrives at the level of his mouth, then lowers her,
which makes nipples slipping between his lips inevitable.

M: "Suck them."

He does suck them, each in turn, even with his intention
known – to lower her, spread her, impale her. Her hands
are buried in his hair, pulling to urge him to keep his
mouth on her body. But she cooperates with the
lowering. His hands, in control of her bottom, spread her
open. His cock juts up perfectly. The lips, 'the lovely
labia' he calls them, the lips of the fine femme fit to the
head, slither on it. At last, hips shudder as the rest of the
lowering engulfs the shaft. Andrés in Mila.

A: "Fuck..."

M: "Yes."

A: "Fuck."

M: "Yes.

A: "So fucking fuck fuck fuck!"

They laugh. Her weight keeps his cock massively shoved
up into her sex. Liquid has been pushed out and drips
down his thighs. Of course they are kissing again, and
laughing and swearing 'fuck' and looking into each
other's eyes alight with wicked, carnal joy.

M: "The boy is strong."

A: "Sex adrenaline."

M: "Don't drop me."

Andrés sobers. Straightens his arms, lifts her off his
shaft. He holds her out, one hand under each mound, the
weight of the woman supported by the power in his
outstretching arms helped by her arms around his neck

pulling up.

M: "Oh shit."

A: "Put your legs up. Over my shoulders."

Incredibly, he can support her while one by one she twists, straightens a knee, eases the heel of the foot onto his shoulder. Andrés leans back at the waist. When both her legs get in place, he pulls her center back in, right over the angry cock, eases her down until she greedily and massively sucks him in all the way to his base. She squeezes. The warm syrupy nectar again, flowing around.

M: "Oh my God, Andrés…"

A: "… like oil inside …"

She can leverage. She can rise a little, then shove down with her weight. She gives him three of these, squeezing as well. Andrés is near the end of his stamina. He manages to carry her three steps, still bent at an angle, to arrive at the side of the table, their eating and massage and … eating table. The bed is too far away. Once again, things go flying off when he lowers Mila to the tabletop, swaying her body to sweep the surface clear. Something flies amok and smashes on the floor.

He surges forward. Her legs around his neck take the force, bend, pull her sex deep onto him. He reaches up and takes an ankle in each of his hands.

M: "Oh no."

A: "Yes."

M: "I can't."

A: "Yes."

M: "No, oh my God."

He urges her ankles high. Way high. She is completely folded in two. Her knees press her torso on either side of her breasts. His organ has penetrated fully. Looking deep in her eyes, Andrés pulls back until only the very tip is within, caressed by the outer lips. For an ineluctable white second, the universe is frozen. Then he drives straight down with all his weight and certainty.

M: "Fucking fuck oh fuck," she screams.

A: "Pull your bottom wide with your hands."

Her left hand fits under one cheek. She uses it to ease the flesh to the side. Her weight on the table keeps the other mound fixed. Andrés feels his seated cock slither and sink another inch into the spread-openness. He pulls out and back. Mila does not hide her eyes from his.

M: "Fuck me."

He rotates from the waist, slamming home, delivering all power and weight. She bellows madly. Another ... and another ... each thrust provoking screams from her throat, each shriek dripping with pitiful begging.

M: "Fuck me. Fuck me. Fuck me. Fuck me.

Andrés delivers one truth intended to slash across her delirious brain.

A: "This is what happens when I can't get your cunt for two days.

chapter 13

deep in the daring

Sunday, June 1, 2014

7:45 a.m.

From The White Sky: After a triumphant breakthrough in sculpting, they shower, twisting under the forceful water, kissing hungrily, laughing and moaning with pleasure from slippery caresses.

She thrashes her wet hair at him.

A: "It's as thick as a mop."

M: "You love my hair."

Andrés puts his right foot square on the bed, leg bent at the knee, lifts her body fully off the sheets, sets it back down with her legs on either side of his solid one. He controls with his left hand in the wet hair. With his right arm around her torso, he shifts her all the way down so the splayed vee presses against his ankle. He has moved her into this position several other times – she knows what to expect.

M: "Wait."

He stops.

M: "You want to pull me by the hair, bind me into position, and make me grind against your leg."

A: "Yes. That's what I want. Do what I say."

M: "Yes. We're going to. But let go of my hair. Take your hands off me."

Andrés considers obeying. She only tries to turn the tables occasionally. He thinks it droll. *Okay, let's see what she can come up with.* He removes all contact. His body reclines on its left side, propped up on the elbow. His right foot remains flat on the bed, planted between her legs. Even so, no contact. He waits.

M: "You like controlling me, Andrés. Grabbing my hair, making me pretend I am bound, telling me I can't talk."

A: "Yes."

M: "You like it when my arms are bound above my head, like this."

She slowly reaches them high up along the bed, crossing her wrists. It tugs her breasts up and exposes her underarms. His cock twitches at the sight.

A: "What are you doing?"

M: "I'm going to give what you like, the sight and sound of me having pleasure, of getting whipped up, groaning, exploding. Andrés likes to make Mila come."

A: "Yes."

M: "You are greedy to give it and see it."

A: "Yes."

M: "And smell it and feel my contractions and taste my saliva and even get my sex juice on your hands and taste me."

A: "Yes, Mila Vovk."

M: "Don't move, Andrés. Do nothing. And do not take your eyes from mine. I am going to give them their fill."

A: "I don't have to do what you say."

M: "Yes, you do."

Andrés breathes faster. Her challenge is brash. He can see in her eyes she is not playing.

M: "Obey me. You are only the spectator. And the hard thing I rub against."

He holds her eyes for several beats of time.

M: "It'll be really hot to watch me rub one off."

She is not backing down. Suddenly the promise of a thrill deep in the daring rushes through him. He feels it like a hot wind that roars. A little piece of irony breaks off: it wouldn't even count as him being controlled ... not if he *lets* it happen. Andrés gives her the faintest nod and agrees with lust in his hooded eyes.

Mila sidles her hips down the bed a few inches. Her thighs wrap around his ankle.

M: "How do you know about using your hard bone on

a woman like this. Did some girl teach you?"

A: "No. I invented it."

M: "I love it. It's you, it's solid, it's perfect. Don't answer. Don't say anything."

A: "Say the 'rub' thing again."

M: "It's going to be hot to watch me rub one off."

With arms still lifted high, resting on the bed above her head, she holds his eyes, and with sweet deliberateness makes her sex rub against the round knob of his ankle. The lips open as if begging for a deep kiss. They are wet. Mila slushes her sex against him in unhurried sensuality. Her legs cross at the ankles, making thighs squeeze. She finds her way, not speaking, watching his eyes as he lusts for the arousal in hers.

Mila arches her back off the bed. The motion pivots her vee against him, and now she can raise and lower her body as well as swivel and press.

M: "It's perfect. It's everything I need," she says, hissing. "Keep watching the pleasure in my eyes."

She increases the intensity of her gaze and slows the pace of her stroking, so she can give him words, like loving insults that heal on the spot.

M: "I can just rub my beautiful cunny like this until I come and come and come."

A: "I like that *cunny* word."

M: "It's not the same as your fucking hard prick slamming into me, ripping in. But a girl loves to rub one off against her clit like this sometimes. It's girly and so fucking good."

She gave a long slow clench. "Mnn. Mmmm. Nmm mm." Then two more rubbing-squeezings.

M: "Another time I'll beg for your mouth on it. Another time I'll shut up and let you fuck the hell out of me. But this rubbing ... I love it."

She begins larger movements. There is a shudder in each cycle. Her breathing races, her skin reddens, her mouth stays open. And her eyes never leave his.

M: "Do you like seeing my pleasure, Andrés?"

A: "Yes."

M: "I'm unbinding one hand."

It descends. The destination is no surprise. One finger of her left hand crooks into vagina, pulling it open so more and more of inner lips are exposed. Another finger pulls the hood away from the glans, then begins a rhythmic push and pull against the tiny sensitive pink dome. All during, the circular rubbing against the hard bone in his ankle never relents.

She escalates rapidly. Andrés sees something familiar and thrilling, a certain flare of the nostrils. He knows this moment in her endgame. He knows she won't be able to speak. But she does -- one more thing.

M: "I give you my pleasure."

Then Mila ascends, fast, violently. So swollen are the tissues between her legs, she can bear a fierce crush of them, seeks it. Both hands grasp his calf and pull her body tight. Then only gripping, and the bellowing that comes with it, and the thrashing wetness that comes with it, and the exploding scent that fills the bed and every ounce of straining joy that comes with her coming, coming.

chapter 14

by the presence
of another

Sunday, June 1, 2014
11:45 p.m.

From The White Sky: The night's sculpting session has ended. Mila looks out over her studio with satisfaction. She nods assent as a final gesture. She flips off the lights. Letting her clay-stained clothes drop on top of his at the edge of the bed, the sight of his arms raised, beckoning, speeds her movements. Then come the first utterances of the night, whispers not audible beyond the bed, each calling the name of the other.

M: "Andrés."
She slips into his arms.
A: "The work ... Mila ..."
M: "Hold me."
A: "You are a great artist."
M: "Hold me."
Her naked body against him pleases warmly, in the soft press of flesh, in the person of the giver, in the body that carries it, in her billowing into his arms. Andrés savors this touching, the embrace of their two naked bodies that exudes affection. It blooms aside from sex just now, delighting on its own. He knows nothing else for a minute. She does not stir.
A: "I liked your fingers touching my face."
M: "I love your chin."
A: "Dented chin."
M: "Yes."
Two minutes of silent breathing pass with no alteration of the delicious affection, skin to skin. It seems hours.

A: "You are melted into me."
M: "I'm not sleepy."
A: "Don't move. I like it."
M: "More than sex?"
A: "Yes. No."

Andrés feels the faintest flicker of something tiny brushing his chest like a feather. She has smiled.

M: "I can't tell if my hand is on your skin right now or on the clay."
A: "Wow."
M: "I want to move it."
A: "No."
M: "What if clay can come alive?"
A: "Let's pretend it can."

More minutes of silence. He becomes aware of their scent, their mixing scents, that of the true persons, accepted unconditionally, warmed to the point of wafting free. This belongs in the ripening olfactory of lovers early in the night, before the sex-scents arrive.

Andrés flips into a trance, its laws quite opposite. He lets it play. In it, Mila's body is a body. He grasps its reality, resting on his torso with weight, moving slightly with their breathing, its heft, its shape -- only this -- there is no woman, no girl. He allows full objectification of the body into focus. He can touch it and move it. He can possess it in many ways. Had it not been given? He can open it for sex any time. Or not.

The power of his will to control explodes in his mind. It shocks him. There is nothing to stop him. Nothing. He possesses a woman. Previously he has been told he has possession, but in this moment the stark truth of it stretches to infinity for the first time. *I possess a woman.* For several long moments he gazes into this reality with no limit and in full rectitude. *Let it run, let it.*

Then, in the distance, a faint shape forms. He struggles to recognize it. How proudly he shines, radiant in the field of his kingly person, yet unable to resist the pull of this new thing. It approaches.

It tumbles into being -- the virtual sensation of a touch on his cheek. It is on his lips, then, and on his forehead at the hairline. There is another touch, at the back of his head.

It is the abstract of Mila's hands exploring him during the sculpting session. At the core of the sensation rests her will. For a millisecond he is astonished to see it – because of the illusion that no will exists but his – and then the shock vanishes. It is Mila's tactile exploration of him, to know him, to move the knowing into her mind and behind it into her heart. He is humbled by the presence of another who seeks him.

He laughs at himself. Discarding the trance with a violent shake of the head, his hands fit to her low back. He sits upright in the bed. Mila remains yielding in her extremities and her core accedes to the movement, letting her sit up and into his lap. Her legs flow around his waist. Andrés pulls her in tight. Their torsos press. Heads go over the shoulder of each other.

They have coupled.

Mila's arms around his neck hold fiercely. His arms on her back pull them together with strength. Everything in the mind and body of each contributes to a gentle rocking, swaying dance that raises the holy ardor with undeniable power, as if under urgency to reassure the gods once again that the humans have found each other in the dark and are making Heaven real.

chapter 15

sex-wise eyes alight and inviting

Monday, June 2, 2014
11:45 p.m.

From The White Sky: Mila is having an off night as an artist – she cannot incite the flow. She circles the sculpture once, carefully. After a profound beat of time in the night, she covers the piece, takes his hand, and leads him to bed.

Mila is in charge. From behind, her hands slide across his skin, reaching around so her arms circle his torso. She embraces with them. Her mouth is not near his.

A: "This is testing me. To surrender."

M: "I know. Let go and let me do."

A: "Are you sad?"

M: "There's a halo of sadness in my heart for my silent hands tonight."

A: "Poetic. How can I help?"

M: "Let me make poetry with my body."

They lay together on the bed.

He increases his surrender by reaching arms above his head, in the way he asks of her so often. Her mouth is on his torso now, hands on his hips.

Her breasts caress. Their pressing becomes deliberate. They tease. She lifts her head to look up at him, but nothing stops the sweet, heavy fall of round flesh and hard nipples against his sex.

M: "Is this one of your dreams? Caresses from your girlfriend's breasts?"

A: "Yes. Sway a little more."

M: "To have a lover who makes love with her lovely breasts?"

A: "Yes."

The deliberateness increases. Mila lets her body fill with eroticism. A coy smile curls her lips and a glint in her eyes contributes.

M: "That first day, on the ferry, you were looking at them."

A: "Did you get mad?"

Mila sits up, straddling him, pressing his cock up against his lower abdomen with her weight. Her hands slowly slide up her torso.

M: "Yes, I got mad. Bastard. Every woman hates that from a stranger. Men stare at your boobs all the time."

A: "Please don't use that word."

M: "Boobs."

A: "It sounds like the stupid teats of a stupid animal. Can you not say it?"

Mila brings her hands to cup them. She doesn't squeeze. She lets the nipples peek out through fingers. Her hips continue to sway, below, and her hands make nearly imperceptible shifts, to move the flesh, change the shape, show how soft.

M: "I like it when you look ... now. I really like it when you hold them like this. And when the tips go in your mouth, Andrés ... I love watching that."

A: "Oh..."

M: "Okay, I won't say that word anymore." She looks down at them. "Goodbye, boobs!"

A: "We can find another word."

M: "Every day, Andrés, touch them like this. And kiss them. Let me see the tips going into your mouth."

She moves her fingers slowly, changing their position. They seem to be both revealing and covering as in modesty. She gathers her hands under and gently lifts. Offering and exposing.

M: "We want our breasts adored. It's not easy for us to keep them erotic. Vulgar behavior on the streets, undergarments that bind, stupid rude names people call them, gravity scary, you can't stop it. We nurse our babies. We worry they'll have a lump. But we still want you to adore them."

A: "I adore them."

M: "We want the person to whom we are given looking at them. We hope you come up behind and put your arms around. We know you only want one thing when you do that. When a man walks up behind a woman, she knows where his hands are going to go. Right then she can use her arms and twist her torso to protect. Or she can arch her back and give them."

A: "Yes. My hands reach around ..."

M: "Touch them, yes. Lift them. Make them bare. Get the nipples hard. Touch them."

A: "Yes."

Mila's hands continue their tender self-caresses. 'Like this,' they say. The sway of her pelvis brings the opposite of tenderness to his cock. She leans forward a little, tilting her wet mouth toward his, her sex-wise eyes alight and inviting.

Andrés lets this dance continue for several minutes. His hands remain extended upward on the bed above his head. Still cradling her breasts in her hands, one of Mila's fingers begins to deliberately slide over one nipple and back, making the puffed areola spring, making the raspberry tip harden and elongate.

Then he moves.

As if in magic, they switch possession. His slides out from under her, slips his body off the bed, spins, and moves her upright on her knees, her back to him as he stands planted on the floor behind.

Mila falls under his command.

A: "Slide your hands down."

They obey. They reach the intersection.

A: "Put your fingers in place."

They find the lips.

A: "Move your legs wide."

They part.

Mila sighs sweetly as she finds the new position. Still kneeling upright on the bed, she leans her head back on his chest. She is surrendered for whatever comes next.

A: "Keep your hands right there. Touch as I enter you."

The head of his organ is in position. He senses the lips and the touch of Mila's fingertips. All is perfect as his weight smoothly surges up and under, until the waiting wet cave is filled.

His mouth stays right at her left ear. From the pleasure-grunts she emits, he knows each thrust tells. Then Mila moans. The thrusts give cruel destruction, one by one, to her privacy and female protections, with each penetration more arrogantly given. She wants the destruction. When all is lain to waste, she burns with lust to give the sweet hurting back, and begins to flex her pelvis to better engulf. She squeezes down with the muscles in her vagina and throughout her lower body. She would snap it off, but everything is so wet she cannot get him fully in her grip to do it.

A: "Put your hands behind my neck."

M: "Oh no."

A: "Do it."

Her arms come flying up and behind. They clasp into place. Inevitably Andrés' hands slide up to take her exposed breasts, cupping, lifting, confining. This is their sexy cleaving, she kneeling on the bed impaled from behind, her body arching, her torso pinned by the massive constraint of his arms, his hands anchoring, so she will not fall forward.

The effect is leverage. The tilted-open sex filled with liquids, the ramrod shoved deep, and all his standing weight and muscles causing absolute freedom for it to pull back, wind up with a surge in his hips and slam back in, the tip brushing against the round cervix far inside.

Normally, Andrés cannot speak during full assault. Nothing must distract the up-flight of his orgasm. This time, he can – and it is she who cannot.

A: "Tease me with them. Let me see down your shirt. Make the nipples hard when I'm not looking, so they poke through."

He stops talking to thrust with total purpose three times. Slamming in. Mila squeals on each.

M: "Oh. Oh. Ohhhh."

A: "Beg me with your eyes to adore them, to caress, to oil them, to suck them. I will."

She moans louder, from his words and his massive plunging.

A: "Make me want to fuck you. And to splash them. To splash your breasts."

His thrusting accelerates. Her increasingly swollen and soaked flesh accommodates the violence. Andrés deliberately makes sounds in her ear that signal his ascent to the top.

A: "Now!"

Mila spins on the bed, uncoupling. Her hands grip his cock, shiny from her wet. Andrés erupts with a deep bellow, a jet splashing against her chest, aimed by her guidance, then another, and with diminishing grunts four, five six more, viscid, carrying the scent of the ocean.

Mila smiles up at him as he stands over her like a king. He has poured his seed over her body. Her hands beautifully and slowly take up the white cream and spread it on her breasts. She gently lifts them and cups them as before, but now each cupful is wet and shiny. Her face is filled with the loveliest of sexual delight, Andrés boils up one more time: a final spurt lands on her left breast.

M: "Adorable."

One finger departs from the others and pulls cream across the nipple. Andrés holds her eyes with his. Between them flashes the most erotic thought possible. Before he can speak it, she speaks.

M: "Next time I'll hold my mouth open and you can splash it in, every drop."

last vestige of
resistance

Tuesday, June 3, 2014
10:35 p.m.

*From The White Sky: Mila Andrés has been shooting
a portrait outside the studio at noon. His sitter departs,
barely reaches the end of the drive before Andrés goes
flying inside seeking Mila.*

M: "Who are you and what do you want?"
A: "Love in the afternoon."
M: "My Latin boyfriend could show up any minute."
A: "He doesn't come here in daylight."
M: "Yes, he does."
A: "No, he doesn't."
Andrés approaches while they banter. She backs away.
She runs out of territory near the doorway of the bed
nook.
M: "I didn't say you could touch me."
A: "I don't need permission."
M: "I'll scream."
A: "If you scream, I'll bind your mouth."
M: "Rude."
A: "I'm binding your hands behind you."
Mila crosses her hands at the base of her spine. It pulls
her shoulders back, lifting her torso. He spins her and
pushes her body against the door.
A: "You can't move. My weight is pressing you into the
door. I'm tying you to it with a rope around your waist.
The rope is rough and tight."
Andrés walks into the kitchen, leaving Mila bound and

pinned by his imaginary ropes. He takes his time getting a drink out of the refrigerator, looks to her frequently. She is struggling against. Twisting. The effort causes harsh breathing.

A: "My hand is at the back of your neck. I'm turning your head against the door. Also, tightening the rope."

The new constraints cause more struggling. She can see him with her immobilized head turned, glares at him with fierce eyes. They grow large when Andrés sets down his drink and walks to her fast. She squirms. He takes his stance exactly behind her body, not touching.

A: "All this twisting is futile. I know how to tie a knot. I like the attempt, though."

M: "Your ropes are insulting."

A: "Were you watching out the window during my shoot?"

M: "Yes."

A: "Did you imagine what would happen the instant I got done?"

Mila shyly whispers 'yes.' A demure confession while bound by ropes. She turns her head to show the corner of her smile.

A: "What was it?"

M: "Oh oh oh he's going to get done with the stupid photography any second, run in here and fuck me."

A: "Exactly."

M: "So insulting you can just do that."

A: "What's it like in your pants, miss?"

From behind, Andrés reaches hands around, unbuckles her belt, unzips the zip of her jeans.

M: "Please don't touch. I'll tell you. I'll tell you."

Andrés applies his weight, crushing Mila against the door, causing her to grunt and gurgle. He is taller than, wider than, stronger than.

M: "Wet. All wet. Leave me alone. Don't touch. It's private. Go away."

His mouth is exactly at her right ear.

A: "You must be kidding. I'm going to put my hand

right down your pants. My fingers in the pudding. Your underwear can't protect you. Why do you even wear it?"

M: "To hold the lips. The mound. To hold me all contained and snug inside my jeans. I like that."

Andrés yanks the jeans to the floor. Mila lets out a shout. Her hands remain bound behind. Andrés curves his hand around her waist, down, under the elastic hem of the garment. His hand fills the vee, fingers slip between lips. Two curl and sink in. The expected moan escapes her throat.

M: "Ohhm oh oh fucking rude hand."

A: "The hand wants what the hand wants."

Mila cannot protect against his control. Her hands are bound. She is tied to the door by rope around her waist. Her legs are separated. With his hand behind her left thigh, he lifts the leg and pins it against the door, revealing the wide space between her thighs, a vault inviting of mystery. Andrés has the leverage, angle, and power to dominate it. He caresses with both hands inside the undergarment, acuity alight with every bit of sex-wisdom in his being. Lubrication increases. His fingers are long, and penetrate deeply. Every time he pulls them out, the pad on his index finger finds the swollen tissue in the roof of vagina, caressing and pressing. That raises lust.

M: "Yes yes yes yes, touch me, yank it, frig me."

A: "Oh, now we change the tune!"

The last vestige of resistance melts. With release of muscles, the spread-open sex lies undefended. Andrés takes advantage with brilliant hands, urges her onward, stroking, penetrating, sloshing with no inhibition. He incites with words.

A: "My hand belongs between your legs."

M: "... my private body. Why is your hand in me?"

A: "You forget how I take. I am hungry Mila."

M: "I feel ravaged."

A: "You like to show off, how wide you can spread, how much juice you can make."

M: "Yes."

He increases the depth of the caressing fingers.

A: "You would open your legs even if I didn't force you."

Silence. Mila hides in the corner.

A: "Even if I didn't force you, you'd open for me, Mila. Mila Vovk, greedy for helpless love."

After a delectably strained moment, with his hand stirring the wet, she whispers.

M: "Yes, Andrés. I open myself for you. For you to see. I love opening for you."

This settles like a prayer over them. He feels the tender touch of it. Then he stirs.

His left hand under her thigh slides the leg several inches up, wedges it against the door, pinning it again. Mila inhales with shock. Somehow Andrés has increased the amount of wide-open girl for his right hand. He invades like a conqueror. The fingers, three now, thrust deep. His hand asserts ownership -- not 'pleasuring her' but rather taking cunt on his fingers.

Suddenly he stops. Mila is heaving. He withdraws his hand. He moves his body away. The girl, balancing on one foot, remains plastered against the door. He lets her hear something in the silence -- the un-belting of his jeans. She cannot see it, but the sound of his garments dropping to the floor causes a whimper in her throat. No other sound or movement for an interminable minute. Her hips sway, pleading, more pitifully the longer nothing happens.

M: "Push your leg one more inch up the wall."

Obeying – he loves the obeying – she slides her left knee. He fits his left knee under hers and pushes up. He returns his right hand to its relentless quest, sliding it around to her front, down into the soaking garment. He grabs the fabric and pulls it to the side, even while one finger eases the lips apart. Using all his strength, his arms lift her bodily off the floor, sliding her up the door.

A: "And the cock wants what the cock wants."

With perfect angle and leverage, Andrés thrusts in from

behind. He pins her to the door with all his weight, with all power of cock. Mila groans – the groans he wants, the pathetic ones that admit he can *ravish* any time he wishes, as deep as he wants, as strong as she fears. Andrés knows all her utterings, the well-fucked up-against-the-wall moaning, the loss and despair sigh.

The *taken* groan.

His thrusting reaches the sexual logos of the woman, the pride of her privacy ... and her abandon. He revels in the out-of-control blubbering, crying, and dirty begging as he invades.

Mila will be strong. Once sure of it, the greed for his orgasm surfaces. Nothing in the way of sensational lust to fuck the woman, just fuck her with abandon, the ache in his groin roaring up with every stroke -- he finds it and flames it, and in the end can feel it his belly and in his lungs when he screams with his mouth in her hair.

a carnal prayer

Tuesday, June 3, 2014
1:05 p.m.

From The White Sky: Mila "Taken and belonging-to during 'time in.' Giving and taking during 'time out," she says. "Which is better?" he asks. Mila laughs and goes slightly shy. She turns her head into his chest so he cannot see. After a moment during which their bodies and hands move gently on one another, she whispers her answer. Andrés rotates above, determined to discover if she were lying.

A: "I'm going to read you a story. It will help you answer which way you like it, taken during 'time in.' Or sharing during 'time out'."

M: "What story?"

A: "I have this book. The lovers in it are like us."

M: "How like us?"

A: "They sex like us."

M: "You just used 'sex' as a verb?"

A: "Yes. Now let me read it."

M: "Don't use 'sex' like that again. It is a noun. Not a verb."

A: "Really."

M: "We do it all day long a million times but it is not a verb."

They lie on their backs, naked, and he pulls a slim volume out from under the mattress.

A: "I'm just going to read one story from this book. The story is called 'Until My Lips Are Sweet'."

M: "Yikes."

Andrés begins:

"No."

That stopped his hand.

Oh, she craved the attempts, the intrusion of strong fingers under her skirt, the persistence to push her thighs apart, yes, this a woman craves from the man to whom she is given. And whom she possesses.

But now she folded up and twisted away, taking refuge in the corner of the car.

"No."

His breathing raced in neutral. No back-off in intent, however. She liked that. Keep trying, was in her eyes.

"Open your legs."

"No."

"Your mouth ..."

"Yes, but that's it."

"Kissing, that's it?"

"You agreed, only kissing."

"Cancel it."

"No."

She liked holding the line, holding him off for play. They would drive to their house by the lake and resistance would vanish. During the drive, she had enticed with subtle bends of the torso and a smile of insincere modesty flashed across. Inflamed by her ripe presence and come-hither glances, he jerked the car onto a side lane. She set the limit at kissing. He agreed — a miscalculation of her oral deviltry. Now he could not stick to the rules. She could hear him thinking — resume kissing only, put a hand under the skirt against the rules, or drive?

Torture.

Her courage rose, buoyed by a challenge of risking he had dropped into the conversation earlier, across a slate tabletop with two wine glasses waiting.

"I have a dare," she said.

"What is it?"

"Put your power away and I'll make the kissing hot. Hotter. Hottest."

"What?"

"Stop trying for more in this car. If you stop, I'll do something hot."

"What?"

"I'm turning off my defenses. If you try for more again, I won't resist. I'll let you take me, right here in this car. We'll climb in the back seat, so you can get leverage, so you can ravage me good."

"Ravage?"

"Yes. Ravage me, destroy me with your member, devastate me with your proud manhood. In the back seat of a car."

He didn't laugh.

"But you'll miss out on my daring secret. It's scary for me. I don't know when I'll have the nerve to do it again."

A frown tightened his brow, as if she were trying to take away his rights or something. Then the brow smoothed.

"Okay," he whispered.

With shields down, she came out of her corner, unwinding and flowing across the seat, tilting her head to give her mouth. He entered it with a moan in his throat.

Behind closed eyelids, the kiss erupted. His lips and tongue roamed with authority. He circled, licking the inside of her cheeks, forcing his lips under her tongue, sucking her liquids into his mouth. Then, he sank deeper. She understood – to dominate an orifice not denied. Her throat and jaw relaxed to let him. A carnal prayer rose in her imagination.

Make me pay.

Her mouth flooded as wet kisses turned to syrup. He put more in, merciless. She held the back of her mouth closed, not wanting to swallow a drop. He stirred the juices, roamed the flesh inside, taking it, marking it, drinking it.

She had never taken a kiss this extreme, never in all their time, never since she gave herself into his eroticism the day they mated for love for good.

A whimper escaped, and a shudder through her body. She backed out. She looked deep in his eyes and swallowed, then parted lips so he could see in.

"All gone. I drank it. All gone."

"More," he said, moving in.

"Wait. I have a better way. Here comes my part of the dare."

She moved out of his arms to the window on her side of the car. Glancing at him once, she put her fingers at the hem of her skirt and drew it up above the waist, revealing bare legs and a white garment tucked snuggly in the delta. A corner of her mind sensed the provocation, knew he might charge in – she would not set vigilance against it, would not resist if he lunged.

She put her fingers in the waistband of the garment and slid it down to her ankles. Revealed in the dim light, the trimmed tuft of hair and below it the tempting wavy line, topped by a tiny bud. Her hand covered the vee. Thighs parted. Two fingers disappeared.

Then, gracefully, the hand lifted away and turned in the moonlight. They saw wetness glimmering. She moved the fingers to the lips of her mouth, brushing across them until liquids transferred. Her lips glistened.

She turned to show him.

"Don't kiss me yet," she said. "I want to make my mouth wetter. More juice until my lips are sweet."

This time she didn't look down, holding his gaze instead. When the hand returned to her face, she gave out little sounds of arousal as the wetness transferred to her lips. She moved separated fingers around her face, touching here and there.

"I love the smell of it," she said, a whisper in the night. "I'll make myself wet this way as many times as you want. Lick me and kiss me." She leaned forward, parted her lips, and offered her perfumed mouth with heartbreaking tenderness.

To her joy, they touch-kissed only, brushing mouths, inhaling. With lips barely parted, fitting and pressing lightly, tiny strings of wetness — her sex wetness — bridged between them each time they lifted off. Once or twice, the tip of his tongue emerged to taste.

"You like me making my lips wet this way, don't you?"

"You'd kiss your own sex if you could reach it."

"Yes, I would," she said. "I'd lick it and drink it for hours."

Three times she renewed the wetness from the source below, each time with more abandon. With the last, with most of her face wet, he roamed everywhere, inhaling, tasting. Finally, he opened her mouth with his and pulled the scent inside, under her tongue, and along the inside of lips. She remained deeply surrendered, and would have taken another of those fat kisses, far, far into her mouth, offering the back of her throat for it.

Instead, he pulled away.

"How am I doing?" he asked.

"Fantastic," she said.

"We're going home now. It'll take half an hour."

She put her hand between her legs.

"Drive fast," she said.

M: "Okay, that's hot. I'm aroused."

A: "I know."

M: "How do you know?"

A: "I can feel you wiggling. I know that lit-up wiggle quite well by now."

M: "Watch out."

A: "Watch out what?"

M: "I want a kiss like that. I want the sex-wet gentle kiss, yeah, but really I want the kiss that goes so deep she cried."

They sit up in the bed. The book slides off onto the floor of the studio.

A: "I asked you a question. Which is better: when you are bound and taken, or when we're giving and sharing with each other?"

M: "Not better. Both, Andrés. Sometimes one,

sometimes the other way."

A: "Okay."

An extended pause. Andrés sees her getting serious. She pulls a sheet around her torso, but keeps her eyes locked on his. Wisely, he waits. Has he gone too far with this outrageous story?

M: "I want a kiss like the one in the story. I'll make my lips wet the way she did. With sex wet. Then put that kiss on me. The one that made her say 'make me pay.' All the way into the back of her throat. So deep it made her cry. Andrés Quevara, someday kiss me like that. Not now, in daylight. Only sometime. You will know when."

A: "Yes. I won't until I will."

They hold eyes for another serious moment. Then Mila lies back down. Slowly she pulls the sheet from her body.

M: "There's an ache in my pelvis now. It's from the story and the way you talk to me. Do you have one?"

A: "Yes."

She holds her arms open to him.

M: "Give it to me."

chapter 18

singing to waves
of pleasure

Wednesday, June 4, 2014
2:35 a.m.

*From The White Sky: After the resurgence of Mila's
drive as a sculptor, they fall asleep. Later, waking,
silence fills the bed. Each lies face up, touching hips,
looking into the night through the skylights. He waits.
It is her moment. "Touch me. Put your hands all over
me. So gentle I faint. Don't stop until I fall asleep
again."*

For long minutes, with no haste, Andrés caresses the
sweet body prone on the bed next to him. It is not a
massage, but rather an awakening of eros. Mila accepts
the touch. Only occasionally a sigh escapes, perhaps as
their eyes meet with affection and longing.

He makes her turn onto her belly. He adjusts the gauge
of touch one step lighter, his right hand easing off until
only fingertips remain on her skin. The feather-weight
caressing with them, delicate and slow, raises gooseflesh.

M: "Oooh. No. No."

A: "Breathe into it."

Andrés does not relent. Mila gradually surrenders,
hissing until she grows accustomed. Her breathing quiets.
His fingertips roam. After many minutes, he has visited
every inch of her back and the exposed sides of her torso.
At the very base of her spine, he slows even more. All
fingers but one lift off her skin. The index lightens its
contact until barely perceptible. It moves with sublime
slowness onto the mound of her bottom.

M: "Oh oh oh."

A: "Lovely and round."

M: "You are evil."

A: "Don't talk."

Incredibly, he finds one more shift of sensibility. Now only the very tip of the pad of his index finger touches. He imagines he only contacts the fine hairs, nearly invisible, or perhaps non-existent, that cover her flesh. A breath would be heavier than this. That thought incites – he begins to direct his exhale.

Mila cannot remain quiet. A rhythmic sweet cooing begins, as if singing to waves of pleasure as they arrive from her libido's soft center. Andrés touches the round bottom everywhere. He does not part any folds of flesh. Eventually he arrives at the back of her thighs. She begins to quiver.

A: "Turn over."

She keeps her legs closed while following this order. They do not miss the ability to hold each other's eyes, finally.

A: "Have you been opening yourself and finding the sweet spot?"

Mila nods.

A: "May I see? Show me."

Prone on the bed, Mila bends at the waist, knees straight, and gracefully lifts her legs far up, reaching toward her left shoulder. No hands – they stay flat on the mattress. As expected, Andrés sees the inviting bulge, puffed up between thighs.

Mila pauses.

Their eyes lock.

She bends at the knees. The legs part. He sees in her eyes the delicious, deliberate quest to move just so, just so to find deep exposure. After a second or two of swaying, Mila's eyes close slowly, lidded with arousal. The swaying stops. Then the heavy eyes open.

M: "Right there."

Andrés shifts his body. His hand moves toward the

offered yoni.

"I wish to touch."

Mila nods.

He thrills with the sensation of slipping into the aura of it, the penumbra of her entire sexual being. He touches the corporal flesh. The wise index finger resumes its discovery. Mila accommodates caresses on the inside of her thighs, then along the crease between thigh and torso. Despite the torture, she bravely maintains exposure, swaying her legs and hips as the locus shifts.

The padding finger slips along the outer lips. It does not penetrate. The transit up and down, twice, three times, again, brings moans from her throat and glinting moisture from inside-out of her sex.

The delicious touching of all her skin has sensitized her triggers. She is already high up. She requires no violent stroking to ascend. The pad of Andrés finger arrives at the pulsing pink button above the opening. He knows exactly where to put it. Where to slip it against. Where to urge it up. There is a hunger to take it in his mouth, yet he does not.

There is no clenching. No penetration. No thrusting or rubbing, only the light contact upon the ripening glans, yet the entire pelvis shivers, then wracks with contractions, accelerating, growing in power. Mila releases her voice with a deep bellow. She lifts it to the skylights. Andrés' hand fills with her flooding juices. He lovingly bathes her vee with them even with her orgasm still raging, beautiful in its exposure, knowing full well the female waters cannot extinguish any fire found there, for long.

between kisses
he whispers

Wednesday, June 4, 2014
7:05 a.m.

From The White Sky: Andrés conducts a photography session of Mila. Nude. They are about to part for several days. She takes a step towards him. Their eyes grow sober. Then – a certain hot glance, like a re-lightning bolt. "Time in," Mila whispers.

Mila is naked.

Andrés, dressed in brown cotton pull-over shirt and jeans, walks from his camera, circles behind to tower over her frame. He loves getting behind her. And to tell her what to do.

A: "Don't move and don't say anything."

He puts both hands in her hair, caressing slowly as if rinsing it in the shower. He gently cranes her head forward and gathers up the thick tresses, pulling them into a crude ponytail, lifting it to expose the nape of the neck. They have been here before.

A: "I'm going to possess you from behind."

M: "I can't see what's coming."

A: "That's right. You should be taken from behind."

M: "What happened to you wanting to look in my eyes during sex?"

A: "You are not ready for that, Mila."

M: "What if I am?"

A: "I'm taking you from behind now."

He stops contention by dropping kisses right at the

hairline. Her body reacts, twisting to escape from – or amplify – the touch. Wickedly, he imparts only a trace of moisture, only half his lips contacting her neck. Except for his hands in her hair and lips on her neck, his body does not touch hers. Between kisses he whispers.

A: "I like you naked when I have clothes on. To have a naked girl in the room, in case I want her for anything."

M: "Take your clothes off."

A: "No way. I'd like to have an entire day – no – a weekend, you are not permitted to put on even one thing, not even a robe around your body, even when I get dressed, even a tuxedo. Just to have a naked girl hovering around, for me to have."

His kissing reaches the tender slope where neck flows into shoulder. He fits his mouth there. Mila tilts her head sideways to make room. Now he allows more wetness into play.

M: "Kiss me. Kiss me. Kiss me."

Hissing her words now, enthralled.

M: "Kiss me. I adore it there. Kissss ... kissss ..."

A: "Eyes closed. So you can't see what's coming at you from behind."

M: "Oh. Ssss Shiss. Oh Oh Sisss.

A: "You smell wonderful."

His mouth opens wide and wet on her neck. He grasps her by the waist and pulls her body tight against his.

M: "Oh, oh, oh."

Andrés is clothed, but this does not hide his anatomy -- her bottom fits against his thighs and the jut of his erection presses her lower back.

M: "What is that thing?"

A: "I've already had you with it three times since yesterday afternoon. Again, soon."

M: "From behind?"

A: "Yes. You won't see it coming."

M: "I don't want to see."

He continues insinuating the thing, the arrogant cock, rudely against her bottom.

A: "Put your hands behind. Find the zipper."

He eases up the mashing their bodies so she can comply.

A: "Unzip."

Reaching behind, Mila uses one hand to hold the waistband of his jeans steady and the other to pull the zipper down.

A: "Slowly. Go in. There's no underwear."

Her hand finds its way into his pants, grasps the shaft, then fits under.

A: "Bring it out."

She uses her talented hands to ease his organs into the open.

M: "I love it in my hand."

A: "Quiet."

M: "Put it in my mouth."

A: "Quiet."

M: "Please. Right in."

A: "Quiet."

M: "I can't be quiet. I don't care if you hate me, I can't be quiet. You *can* make me shut up, just put it in my mouth. Please. Right in my mouth."

Behind her back, Mila contains his sex with her hands, one around the shaft, one underneath him.

A: "Bend over. Put your hands behind your thighs."

Whimpering with disappointment, her mooing mouth expresses sweet regret that her hands must remove themselves from possession of the phallus.

She bends at the waist.

A: "As far as you can. Pull your breasts against your legs."

Mila's bottom rounds up at him. He slips fingers in the cleft between the puffy lips, easing them apart. The tip of his cock lowers into place. He lifts his left foot onto a bench nearby, forming a crouching, powerful position with leverage.

The thrusts begin.

A: "This is what the naked girl is for. She is always ready."

He keeps thrusting while talking, slipping lusciously into the exposed girl, hands around her waist pulling when he slams forward, so the penetrations rip in hard.

A: "She has the wet box, she has it, I just tell her to expose, she opens it wide."

He can say no more. His thrusts into the bent-over woman -- who gives herself like a perfect miracle -- enrage his senses. The magnitude of sex, exquisitely given, stops his consciousness. He can only rampage like a buck, to prove he has it.

One of her hands pulls her breasts tight against her thighs, the other curls around his ankle on the bench, to anchor her body as a solid target.

She cannot obey the order to be silent. She absorbs each blow without grunting, a beautiful insult to his power, but her fluttering high voice is free.

"Oh la la oh hhho ..." gurgling and squealing bright.

She does not rise up to orgasm. Bent over, spread apart, taking his giant ramrod slamming into her sex, Mila twists her torso to look in his eyes. She aims a sharp arrow.

M: "How far away? It's in your pelvis, in your ass, in your stomach, isn't it Andrés? I want it. Let it build, then blast it into me. How far? Thirty more strokes? Ten? A hundred? Fuck it into me."

Mila screams as he doubles the violence of the thrusts, savagely, like trying to slam her voice into silence. After two vicious ones that nearly knock her to the floor, she finds her voice again.

M: "I have the wet box ... all slick ... slosh around ... I have so much juice you don't even know."

Three more wild thrusts, making her grunt and squeal on each.

M: "... pissed off you didn't put your cock down my throat."

It causes a hesitation. Into it she unloads, in extremely low voice ripe with intent.

M: "So just shove it up my fucking cunt."

The blinding dirty beauty of the word from his sweet happy lover sends him to the brink of coming. She is not far behind. Together they grunt and scream and slam against each other until they go off, collapsing on the floor of her studio into a wet spot, the warm pool of their together juices.

chapter 20

only one small protest

Friday, June 6, 2014
10:55 a.m.

From The White Sky: Forty-hour-reunion sex.

Andrés roars up the drive and slams to a stop outside the studio. If he thinks he is going to unleash his two-days-no-sex caveman drama of total control, he is destined to reconsider. Mila greets him naked, pulls him across the room, and begins to yank off his clothes. Her person is alive with arousal, a delightful greed bubbling. She is aggressive. Andrés could quash this role reversal, but no, maybe not, go with the erotic mission of a woman crazy to have him. Who could possibly wish to derail that?

They tussle for control next to the bed. The confluence of voracious mouths -- both try to kiss at the same time – is both arousing and ridiculous.

A: "Stop trying to run it."

M: "Equal."

A: "Let go."

Mila resists more, grabbing his jeans, already loosened, yanking them down to the floor. She yanks his undergarment as well. Then she is on her knees yanking ... him.

M: "Yes! The thing of the cowboy. The ding-dong thing. My proud possession!"

Roaring loud, Andrés reaches down, grabs her under her arms and pulls her upright. Just in time. A split second later and his organ would have been buried in her mouth. There might have been injury.

Their eyes meet. Defiance. Then the battle resumes, mouth to mouth. He cannot get her under control. Her mouth keeps rejecting his when it tries to invade. He tries three times. He pulls back, breathing hard. Mila flashes her eyes at him, triumphant.

A: "Put your hands behind your back."

M: "No."

A: "I'm binding them behind"

M: "No."

Inspiration blows through. It is so clever, he shakes visibly for a second.

A: "Time out."

M: "What?"

A: "Time is now out."

M: "You can't call time out."

A: "Oh yes I can. Time out."

He has rendered her frozen. Andrés reaches down and takes his jeans in hand. Lifting them ... the sound of the belt buckle rattling. With his fingers on the buckle, he lifts his eyes to her face, to watch the reaction. With a deliberately slow tug, he pulls the belt from the garment. Mila's eyes go huge.

M: "Oh no you don't."

A: "You need to be bound for real."

M: "Oh no you don't."

A: "It's not to hit you. It's to bind you."

M: "No."

A: "Then put your hands behind your back, be bound, so I can take you any way I want."

M: "No."

A: "Then you need to be bound for real. I can't have you able to refuse, I need to control. I need to bind you for real. Time is out, so we can discuss it. Change the rule. Allow it."

A starkly beautiful moment of terror. Mila stops breathing. Andrés stands before her, strong on the floor with feet spread apart, adamant, belt in hand.

M: "Not to hit?"

A: "Never."

M: "Then yes. Yes. Yes. You can bind me for real."

A: "Say what I need you to say."

M: "Time in."

To the exquisite chagrin of her female self, Andrés conducts a gigantic escapade of pleasure on Mila Vovk, hands bound behind by his belt, the actual leather belt of his pants. She has been tossed into the bed and contained, helpless against the onslaught. Even if she wants to kick, she dare not try – he could bind her legs for real, perhaps with rope, tie them spread wide.

The most thrilling aspect runs on as orgasms course through her body – the illuminable awareness that even though she could, she must decline with bottomless surrender to say 'time out' to get the belt off. Through eyes full of rapture, she sees that Andrés knows how helpless she is to say it, that her heart is broken -- broken open with letting.

She manages only one small protest.

M: "I thought when you bound me for real it would be to use me like a thing."

A: "No."

With his fingers, with his mouth, and with his triumphant cock, he makes her come many times.

chapter 21

interrupt with kisses

Saturday, June 12, 2014
6:55 a.m.

From The White Sky: The sun emerges and lights the bed of Mila and Andrés through the skylights, the indirect north-angled slant beautifully soft. They stir slowly. Six hours thick sleep for both is unusual and a victory. They rise and say something about food, but this choice falls to second place. Sex beckons louder.

In the bathroom, they decline a shower, even though Mila's skin carries a faint sheen of massage oil. The natural scent of each, inhaled deliberately when they press bodies together, gives pleasure, and they do not wish to wash this away. They stare at each other while brushing teeth. The final rinsings do not take away the strong zing. They join mouths to share it back and forth.

Then they walk back to bed.

M: "Please. Not rough."

A: "I'm still loaded up. Happens when I can't get you for two days. Let go. Let me."

M: "Please, Andrés, no."

His counter argument, ready on his lips, would be to announce she is indeed strong enough to receive his control. Instead, like a healthy decision not to eat two desserts even though no one would catch him gorging, he relaxes.

A: "Okay."

M: "I want to talk and kiss."

A: "I want to touch your breasts."

M: "Are we too cute?"

A: "The massage and sleeping together like spoons, that

was so cute."

M: "Yes. Cute like a girly fantasy."

A: "But before that, with the belt ..."

M: "Stop. Don't talk about it. That was ... big. I don't want to talk about it."

A: "Okay."

Mila holds up her wrist. They inspect the indentations and scratches on it. She drops it to the bed and they move on.

M: "Raana is jealous of me."

A: "Because of your art?"

M: "Very funny. You know better. It's because I have a cool boyfriend and she doesn't. She kept bringing it up in Boston."

Mila and Andrés spend unknown time for pillow talk. She does most of the talking. They interrupt with kisses, occasionally. She makes a show of allowing the insinuation of his hand onto her 'bosoms.' She says yes, in a whisper, when he puts his hand there. It makes her talk about underthings.

M: "Veronica couldn't help herself. She wandered into a really expensive lingerie shop on Boylston. Before she realized what she'd done, she got furious and stomped out. I tortured her by lingering inside while she fumed outside."

A: "Cruel."

Eventually, the closeness warms them. The kisses become more frequent. They become open. At a certain ripeness, Mila shifts her hips and slides on top, the boy readiness ... readily apparent.

M: "Please. Please let me."

Once again, he relaxes. Mila grasps the hard erection. She rolls her wet sex onto it. She closes her eyes. She slides up and down several times to engorge everything. She positions to make the tip find the opening. She lets her weight tell. She begins the sensual dance that has the delightful denouement.

Occasionally, Mila slows, and they say gentle things to

each other. They smile while joined. They try to figure out what pet name to call her breasts. Then, she resumes her sweet squeezing and sliding.

It is pillow-talk sex.

chapter 22

primitive, dirty, erotic

Saturday, June 7, 2014
7:55 p.m.

From The White Sky: They are having a dinner-date, with promise of dancing after. Between courses, Mila becomes suspicious.

"Where's the dance floor?"

"I like your hair like this."

"We're not going to some bar, are we?"

She know there is no club for ballroom dancing on the island.

"With your hair up and shoulders bare, I am enjoying the view." He stops her with that comment. It is a perfect moment for a public display of erotic affection.

Mila very prettily lets go of her investigation and takes up the compliments.

M: "I see your eyes on me."

A: "I'm good at it. No one can tell I'm leering."

M: "What if I start to blush?"

A: "You are an artist and prance around naked all the time. You have no shame and have probably not blushed since high school."

M: "I'm uninhibited. But sometimes I like to put on modesty anyway, for girl privacy."

A: "Like undies under a dress that no one can see?

M: "Yes."

A: "That I can take off?"

She stops. In her face, he sees his words strike home. Andrés leans across the table and whispers.

A: "I like you having privacy, secrets, little erotic dreams, underground memories. I want to find them. Uncover them."

M: "Don't touch them."

A: "You probably have more than you think. I have them too. And we can invent new ones. Give one of yours to me."

Mila shakes her head.

A: "Give one to me. Now."

M: "What?"

A: "Trust me."

M: "You scare me."

A: "Yes. We are having an erotic moment right here in the dining room of the Harbor View. You should be scared."

M: "I don't want anyone else to see."

A: "Trust me."

Mila's breathing accelerates.

A: "Close your eyes."

She holds her head steady, eyes closed.

A: "Do what I tell you."

She nods.

A: "Now, invent something. A secret. Specific. Something that turns you on, but that you would never let anyone know, including me, out of modesty."

Her breathing quickens. Lips part slightly. Andrés adores her with his eyes to an extreme, now she is not looking. Her hair, her skin, the slight swell of breasts above the dress. He waits, allowing time for her imagination to churn. He looks around to be sure no one else can detect their intimacy.

A: "We look normal. No one can see your secret. Hold it close and precious. I am not going to ask what it is. Ever. But you are going to show it to me without words."

The tiny flare of nostrils, the crinkle between her eyes. He pauses to let the tension build.

A: "Now. Open your eyes. Let me see it."

Mila appears proper from a distance for a public room. Yet to him, her lover, she exposes all. All.

A: "Let me see."

They are wet, the brown eyes that look in his. And from her face to her throat down across her chest, heaving more than normal, her flesh blushes bright.

A: "Are you in it right now?"

She nods.

A: "Is it sexy?"

She nods.

A: "Don't tell me. Just show me."

They hold each other's gaze for seconds. The fantasy blossoms, runs a story on her artist's imagination. For one flashing instant at its height, she cannot abide – her eyelashes flutter – she glances away. Andrés waits. She turns her gaze back, more intimately exposed then he could have dreamed. Her heat runs its course to the rhythm of her breath, then fades like a dream expiring on a cloud. She takes time to quell her breathing, ending with a sigh.

A: "Don't ever tell me what you imagined."

She shakes her head to agree.

A: "Was it extreme?"

Mila nods.

A: "Deep in your erotic heart, with your privacy wrapped around it."

She cannot say a thing. That thrills him. To render her mute, it must have been primitive, dirty, erotic.

M: "That was like a slow dance, pressed up against someone you may or may not sleep with for the first time."

A: "But that was not the exact image."

M: "No."

chapter 23

must taste each other

Saturday, June 7, 2014
9:00 p.m.

From The White Sky: They are slow-dancing in a private room. There is no way to pull closer – their bodies are already melted into each other's. When the music resumes, it continues to be dancing, but barely. All the usual dance-steps cease, while the subtle and loaded pressing of one body into the other, a sweetness all lovers know, grows in urgency.

M: "I wish I were taller. I want your mouth on mine, but I don't want to move."

A: "Go up on tiptoe, we'll rub together. On the way down too."

In sweet simmering moments like this, they want affectionate kissing -- sweet and simmering. But sometimes they fall straight through to sex kissing. There may be no warning.

She tries going up on tiptoe. The up is delicious. The arrival of her mouth magical. It tilts to fit him. It is warm, yielding and filled with wetness when he puts his mouth in it. She lets him sink deep, relaxing, opening herself with unashamed abandon.

Drink me, she says with her entire body. *Don't miss a drop, don't stop until you push the flesh of my mouth apart to find nectar I am holding deep in. I hold my mouth wide open and tilted up so you can drink the juice, all of it.*

His left hand moves her head back and forth, which

helps him ease in. Just as he believes no woman could let herself be kissed this deep, more of her throat opens. He knows she is using body-wisdom learned from taking his phallus in it. Her hand fits to the back of his head and pulls him forward, deliberately urging him in.

This carnal devour lasts the entire song, so intense they stop dancing. The only movement: his mouth inside hers, slowly rocking back and forth, with lips and tongue at the opening of her throat.

As the last strains of King Cole fade away, Mila comes down off tiptoes. He slips out of her mouth. As she eases down, the sliding of her breasts against him seems deliberately effected. She does not show her eyes to him, a coy modesty to veil the brazen act her mouth has performed. She ends in her former position, head on his chest.

It is their most erotic oral act.

Elvis says: "Wise men say, only fools rush in, but I can't help falling in love with you." They resume swaying to the music.

M: "Andrés?"

A: "Yes?"

M: "That kiss went all the way down."

A: "I know."

M: "I can feel the lips between my legs slipping together now. Wet. Because of that kiss, your mouth inside mine. I'm wet."

A: "Oh my God."

M: "I'm squeezing."

A: "I never dreamed we could kiss that deep."

M: "I'm learning how, more every day. Learning how to open my mouth and throat for you."

A: "We can't go back to our table. People will see how hard I am."

M: "I want them to see. They have never seen a woman open herself like that. They were watching me. Never seen a man sink his mouth that deep in hers. They know it is sex. I'm proud of being able to kiss like that, making you hard. Let everyone in this ballroom see you rubbing it against me."

He shifts slightly. She moves her hips so the spot right under her belly pillows it. They begin to exaggerate the dance-swaying. This strokes him through his clothes. So skilled is this performed, it tugs him up to maximum erection.

M: "Again," she whispers, and rises up on her toes, sliding against.

Andrés has danced them close to the music equipment. He clicks onto the iPod and hits 'pause,' rotates back face-to-face with Mila, looks into her eyes, then tilts his head opposite hers. He moves his right hand onto her neck. Thumb and index finger fit themselves under her chin, the better to feel movements in the throat. The other hand stays at the back of her head. Thus, he holds the head cradled, but the control is implied, not tangible.

Mila understands. She eases her body away from his and bends her arms behind her back, hands enfolding themselves as if bound together. The only touch remaining: his hands holding her head. It is a thrilling act of surrender.

Lips meet. The expected penetration does not occur. Instead, he seems only to desire the flesh of the lips alone.

A: "Don't open your lips."

He presses gently and releases, to test the resiliency. He puts the tip of his tongue under and pulls gently, then let's go, to assure they belong to him. He turns the underside of his lips on hers, wetting them. There, there, using the moisture of his mouth, he wets her lips. She holds them offered for it, lips pressed together so no drops of the fluids can disappear inside. He wants the flooding. Wants her face wet.

He pulls back to look at her lips. They do not move. His hands hold her head steady, her commitment to his control absolute. The lips are prominent, swollen slightly and glistening. Under the glaze of wet, they shine pink, not red. He falls in love with every wrinkle, with every curve, with every color of Mila's lips. They will part instantly, he knows, if he orders them to, and the wetness will fall into her mouth. They echo the other lips, the ones also wet right now, he is sure, which will also open when he orders.

He shifts his eyes to look in hers. The deep acceptance, the absolute alert sensitivity to her 'letting,' the beauty of the woman he loves shining in them.

A: "Your mouth and lips and face are really wet. Don't lose any of it. I want it back now."

She nods carefully.

Andrés lowers his mouth over hers. He slides his insides across Mila's closed lips. He uses the lips as he uses her nipples when kissing her breasts, as a firmer prod in his mouth when roaming soft female flesh. He seals his mouth around hers, then allows maximum release of wet from his own glands to fill the interior. When he moves back and forth, holding her head rock steady with his hands, a film of wet escapes and slicks the surfaces of her face. He roams far with this, wetting her chin, her nose, her cheeks.

They have earned this intimacy. Their juices belong to each other. They cannot be without them blending for long. They must taste each other.

M: "I want that extreme kiss now, Andrés. The one in the story you read. Can it be even deeper than we just did?"

A: "Yes."

M: "May I have it now?"

A: "The other wetness should be on your lips."

Mila nods to him, vulnerable and risky. Her hand slips between her legs, seeking the lubrication secreted there. She lifts her wet fingers to her mouth, caressing slowly with Andrés watching everything. She slows the touch of her fingers, then holds the anointed lips up to him, offered.

M: "Make me pay."

chapter 24

like whispers would be

Saturday, June 7, 2014
11:00 p.m.

From The White Sky: **Andrés** *and Mila are in a hotel cottage for the night, dancing and touching. He has been whispering romance in her ear, with permission to be extreme in poetry ...*

M: "I can't have sex with this much emotion. Andrés. Don't say anything more. Don't kiss me like that. Enough ... all I can take."

A: "I think –"

M: "Don't talk. Please. Your talking is too much. No talking."

Andrés removes her dress. Her undergarments are amazing, from an expensive shop in Boston. Mila will let him remove nothing else, bouncing away from his hand. He must slowly seduce her, limited to light kisses, with a hand on a silk undergarment here and there.

He tracks her to a wall across from the bed where a mirror reflects the full length of them. He spins her around to face it.

Holding his arms straight out, palms flat on the mirror, feet spaced wide apart, he hopes to confine her. She is small and quick -- he keeps his hips ready to attempt a block if she flees. But Mila places her hands on the mirror too. Very slowly, to not alarm the quarry, he brings his body in contact with hers from behind. She is not skittish – she sways back against him from shoulders to bottom.

Andrés and Mila press and rub. He is still fully clothed,

she naked except for the two minimalist garments that cover little and say much. The play of their eyes into the mirror, sometimes glancing in each other's, sometimes on bodies, serves quite well in substitution for speaking. Eloquent. Heating. Penetrating, like whispers would be.

Eventually Andrés risks his hands. She keeps hers flat on the mirror. She has understood this necessity. His hands, then, touch her flesh.

Mila takes the touching. She does not close her eyes. She does not flee. She allows the unfastening and removal of the garments that had protected her modesty. Now she wears only her nakedness. Andrés roams it with hands.

Eventually he risks bigger moves. His hands fit behind her knees. He lifts her off the floor, folding her in half until her thighs press her abdomen. He can hold her aloft and secure with one arm and hand. His other loosens his gray trousers just enough. In a power move, he bends backward in an arc, gently lowers her to the point of joining up. He stops.

Mila understands. Her hands find his hard organ. She aims it with one hand, separates her lips with the other. They make the joining.

For as long as Andrés can sustain the weight, they rock together in this position. The contrast between her soft nudity and his rough clothing excites. But the stance cannot last. Their movements speed up and they gradually sink to the floor.

There in front of the mirror, with many glances into it during, they make love on the rug of their lovely room at the harbor of the lovely town near the sea. Their ascent, slowly, together, while looking in the mirror, with him behind and over her body, seems so sweet and fulfilling, they believe themselves for a flashing instant never to need more, do more, feel more.

It is the fleeting satisfaction of paradise.

chapter 25

oral

Sunday, June 8, 2014
8:00 a.m.

From The White Sky: **In the hotel cottage ...**
"What time do they kick us out?" she asks.
"I arranged for late checkout."
Mila squeals with delight and rolls over on top.
"Now I'm going to make you blush," she says, looking like
a girl filled with serious Old Black Magic.
She weaves it well.

Mila is oral.
Delightfully, she cannot decide which parts of him need
most attention. Kissing is easiest. He repeatedly finds her
mouth on his.
A: "You kiss like anything."
He recognizes one of his moves, now unloaded on him.
M: "Don't swallow anything. It's a French kiss."
How many times has he used this on her?
Such kisses ripen accord. Each accepts the juice of the
other. Acceptance will quicken to enthusiasm, will grow
to voracious lust, will blossom to passion. If also they
love, this will make them weep with happiness.
Mila permits his hands on her back and neck, allows his
caressing and urging with them. She possesses the
leverage, however. Her body rests atop his, the complete
weight of it pressing home her possession of the play.
She kisses him like anything.
Then, Andrés feels a tear fall on his cheek. Mila stops
kissing, but hides her face, turning her head and to tuck it

along his neck.

A: "Just lay still."

M: "I can't get away from you."

A: "Good."

M: "I want you in my mouth."

A: "Good."

They do not move, except for the rise and fall due to heaving breathing, gradually receding.

M: "It's the most daring thing. To take it in my mouth. But stay innocent."

A: "Yes."

M: "I ache to."

Andrés does not respond. Perhaps struck dumb by the realization of holding in his arms a woman who cares about her innocence while drenched with sexual heat. He waits, admiring the grim courage. The morning grows brighter in their wonderful room, the brass of the bed glinting gold. They lie in a bower of white sheets and pillows, benefiting from a light breeze off the ocean flowing through one window he cracked open. He savors the taste of Mila in his mouth from her liquid kisses.

Then she moves.

Her hair is wet. It trails across his chest. Her hands roam his torso as she slips down his body. Mila presses with her breasts deliberately. Her transit slows as if for drama, arrival drama, destination worthy, and she stops with the tip of the man at the lips of her mouth. Andrés cannot see because of her thick brown hair spread across his abdomen in disarray. Her hands settle on his ribcage.

As perhaps never before in life, his soul floats serene in reality, his body surrendered deeply in the bed, everything quiet, released and beatific ... except for the phallus, the organ, with its vivid penumbra of power. It is enormous in all ways. The erection, belligerent with intent, famished for the orifice one inch away, jerks once, twice, again, in brilliant contrast with the peaceful logos of his being. Both the serenity and the exigency are sublime.

This is his reward for achieving Mila.

chapter 26

simple nude kissing

Sunday, June 8, 2014
11:30 a.m.

From The White Sky: **Mila is recovering from an
emotional break. She is just beginning to care about things
again ... including memory of oral sex a few hours prior ...**

He takes her in his arms and begins kissing, begins
disrobing her, begins caressing her skin as it becomes
exposed. Confidence transits to her from his touch.

A: "Raise your arms."

He lifts her sweater up and off. Mila wears nothing
under it, having jettisoned her bathing suit when
changing clothes in Chilmark. His hands roam her naked
torso.

M: "You like them."

A: "Yes, I do. Do you love them? Your breasts?"

M: "Yes." She is cautiously certain.

A: "Thank goodness."

M: "Why do I think you are going to do something dirty
with them?"

A: "Dirty is beautiful"

M: "I don't want to answer the big questions. I don't
know what to do next. I just know I don't want to be
'what the fuck' anymore."

A: "This is perfect. Because I know what you should do
next."

M: "Really?"

A: "Yes. "Do you want suggestions?

M: "No. Order me around."

Andrés finishes removing her clothing. And his. They are standing next to the bed. The only light comes from the fire and one small lamp. He reclines first, with her watching closely. He offers his hand, guides her into his arms. Two people have gone to bed together. The result is simple nude kissing. Mila has received no orders, so each kisses each, fair and square.

A: "Kissing is loving."

M: "Yes?"

A: "Touching is loving."

M: "Yes?"

A: "I want to watch while you touch yourself."

M: "I like the way you touch me."

A: "How long were you without a someone before me?"

M: "I already told you that."

A: "How long?"

M: "Two years, damn it."

A: "Show me how it was for those two years. How you pleasured."

M: "No."

A: "You don't have my permission to say no."

M: "What the fuck no!"

A: "I want to see your hand between your legs."

M: "See, I knew you were up to something dirty."

Normally, the kidding would escalate. Now Andrés stops it. He does not respond. They lie in each other's arms with ample flesh on flesh, but no movement for many long seconds. They hold each other's eyes.

A: "No joking. No pretending it's dirty right now."

She still says nothing. There are no jokes in her expression, however.

A: "Put your hand on your belly."

It requires the space of four breaths. She does not take her eyes of his, does not smile, does not falter. She places her left hand as directed.

A: "Don't move it."

She gives him the briefest nod of the head to concur.

A: "My hand loves your body, Mila. You let me touch, it is the main thing you let me do, you know the power of touch, it is your fire, to touch, and you have let me so many times, freely, to touch you."

M: "Yes."

A: "Move your hand to where the scar is."

There. To the scar from giving birth.

A: "I love you there."

M: "Me too. It is beautiful."

A: "We know why."

M: "Yes, we know why."

A: "I will give you a fantasy now."

M: "Oh my God."

A: "Move your hand down."

M: "Where exactly, master?"

A: "Let two fingers slip into the cocoon, keep one busy on the cute little bud."

M: "I like your names for it."

A: "Caress how you did for two years. Don't stop caressing."

M: "Okay. Let's see if I remember."

A: "Hilarious. I'm going to kiss your mouth. In the kiss ... I need to put into it what we did this morning, it was only this morning, before we left the Harbor House. What you allowed. What you did. With your mouth."

M: "It was ..."

A: "It was not dirty. It was sublime. I have never felt that beautiful, guy-beautiful."

M: "What is my fantasy?"

A: "Don't stop your hand."

Mila is not without power to bend his rules. She draws her left hand up and presents it. As her fingers move and separate, strands of her juice span and slip over them. After a moment, her hand falls back between her legs.

A: "I didn't tell you to do that."

M: "No, you didn't." She smiles coyly.

A: "Your hand knows what to do."

Smiling broadly, she nods with female wisdom on

display.

A: "The fantasy I'm giving you is to replay. In the kiss.
Replay."

M: "You mean ..."

A: "We both replay this morning. But in our kiss."

She has stopped breathing.

A: "When you took my erection in your mouth."

M: "Oh. Oh."

She needed that piece of anatomical clarity. They each
thrived on poetry, but occasionally needed to strip the
poem away.

A: "I'm going to kiss you while your hand is making you
come. And that's what we will be thinking about the
whole time. When you let your mouth open and took my
cock in so sweetly, and let it slip down into your throat."

"Andrés ..."

A: "I once warned you this was going to happen."

M: "I remember."

A: "Now."

They are perfectly positioned on the bed. Comfortable.
Mila's left hand definitely knows what to do between her
legs. Her head tilts slightly as Andrés brings his mouth to
hers. Everything turns wet and hot.

He knows she is complying. Her mouth surrenders
under his. This must be how it was, for so long, for the
many engulfings she performed, so slow and gentle,
sometimes half way – and he now kissed her like that –
sometimes taking him all the way in. Andrés kisses her
only to experience the flesh of her remembering and
forming up as it had.

Unexpectedly, the reenactment becomes very real. The
sensation fills his entire body. This must be because he
has not erred, Mila had given herself this morning so truly
that now he feels the same reaction in his back, his pelvis,
and his cock. He presses it against her thigh to complete
that circuit.

Inside the kiss, a steady beat faintly emerges. It is the
reverberation from the rhythm of her hand at her sex,

stroking, tugging and slashing. A small guttural cry fills her throat on each beat. These he devours. Everything accelerates. Mila reaches the crest, easily in sight of the top. He pulls his mouth from hers and whispers right into the beginning of her orgasm.

A: "I've never known such pleasure, Mila. I felt your sorrow and your beauty. And your love."

He slips his mouth back inside hers. Her spasms begin. He feels her legs quaking. Mila's other hand fits to the back of his head and pulls, urges him deeper into the kiss. That is extreme. Where a woman wants to cry out, she does so, but violently inside his mouth, not into the freedom of the air. Andrés swallows it all.

That is his last image. How it must have been, this morning, at the end, when she took his explosion in her mouth.

chapter 27

she understands this dance

Monday, June 9, 2014
10:00 p.m.

From The White Sky: They have been telling each other origin stories. It has exhausted Mila.

He lays her body face-up in bed.

Andrés asserts control that is no more than him being in charge. There is little resistance in Mila, no more than her acquiescence. Their moves are beautiful, a languid ballet.

A: "Receive."

M: "I'm receiving."

He extracts her arms from the robe and arrays them straight out perpendicular to the torso, her legs straight down the bed. Under the kind lighting, her skin, with the first strata beneath, refracts and scatters the light, producing a translucence of both otherworldly illusion and natural-seeming flesh.

Mila is nude and offered.

Andrés touches at will. The muscles along the fingers perform no grasping, and those at the wrist no in-gathering. His hands set themselves here and there ... and melt. Yet ... Andrés' hands claim they belong touching the body of the woman – that is the claim. No quiver, no flinching, no gasp of breath will gainsay his sureness.

M: "Warm."

A: "You are warm?"

M: "They don't burn."

A: "What don't?"

M: "Your hands. Your touch. Only warm. They don't burn me."

Andrés uses solely his right hand now. It arrives on the outside of her left hip. In graduated steps, he transits down her thigh, then – at her knee – slips behind to fit in the crook of it, still not grasping. He requires many shifts of the quiet hand to find each subtle place that must be touched, there. His eyes glance up to find hers. They affirm he must continue to search this place, behind the knee. His shifting slows, until the belief they have not ended becomes a test of both their sensibilities.

Mila invokes a deep breath, a sure release. Andrés' hand moves on. Her calf. Her ankle. Her foot. Both feet with both hands now. The touching of them without grasping is so contrary it provokes an ache they both feel, as if the torture of a kiss that does not kiss. Gradually, at the height of it, all movement stops. The last is that of his eyes, which find hers.

A: "Don't move your arms."

Andrés uncoils from his position at the bottom of the bed and slides his body along hers. His arms slip underneath to embrace the woman into them. His hips sink into the space between her legs to gently ease them apart, the insinuation of his organs guided by the utter confidence of knowing the way. Andrés slides into Mila perfectly.

No thrusting. Andrés stays embedded, and ceases all movement. They are eye to eye on the bed. Then, like a dancer making changes, he removes his member, and comes to the next position, head resting on her abdomen, his slicked cock pressed against the inside of her right calf. They breathe together into it.

The next finds the entirety of his body out of the bed, kneeling on the floor, his face buried in her right hand. Mila does not move her fingers against his lips. She understands this dance.

Then his lips are at her hairline. On her right side. His body remains outside the bed. Andrés kisses along the edge of her face, where brown hair begins. They are precise, whispering kisses. A tiny tremble in her shoulder tells him she is imperfect in the abeyance of display. The arousal exists, the shudder says.

A: "Cross your right hand over to your left hip."

He waits until she settles. Then he pauses until a beat of his dance passes in silence. Then, in one smooth motion, he eases onto the bed, wedges his left hip under her right and, with the help of upper body strength, rotates Mila onto her left side, with his body fitting against hers from behind. They hold like this for one, two, three beats.

A: "I am hard as a rock."

This provokes a giggle from the girl with the male organ slammed against her lower back.

M: "Put it in me again."

A: "No."

M: "It's throbbing."

They laugh well at this purple word they have never uttered in their lives. Either of them.

A: "What is throbbing?"

M: "My vagina throbs to have you in it."

His lips at the back of her neck kiss slowly. That is the full extent of his next move. The intimacy they have established while kissing *right there* in previous lovemaking comes home – surely she is now burning.

Andrés executes a long drop down the spine of Mila, then, with his mouth wet against her skin. Of course, he does not hurry. Apparently, every vertebra must receive attention. Mila bravely holds position during this tortuous run.

At the base of the spine lies the sacrum. This triangle at her lower back is not unknown to Andrés. His mouth begins its visit. As the tiny kisses flow, his right hand enters the dance. It gently finds the crook behind Mila's right knee and fits into place. He stops everything. His lips hold against her skin.

Then the drama grows serious. His right hand pushes her leg up toward her torso. Her leg bends at the knee, but this does not stop the hand from control. Andrés is opening Mila.

A: "Put your right hand behind this knee. Pull it all the way up."

Now Mila is opening herself. There is separation between her thighs as the right leg is lifted out of the way. Andrés' right hand is free. He waits until Mila has pulled her leg all the way up and thus spread the space between her thighs wide. She holds still.

His right hand slips onto the vee. The lips of her sex sit in the palm of his hand. The matchup, the fit, is so ideal one wishes to know the selections nature made to accommodate the perfection of it. Andrés loves his hand there. Between. Cupping. Holding preciously.

M: "You have me."

A: "Yes."

M: "How long are you going to touch me like this?"

A: "You will let me do it forever. So you don't need to know."

He himself ... does not know. His possession by holding now becomes possession by gentle caress, and now he thinks the answer is indeed 'forever,' because the sinking in, the discovery of smooth flesh softened with her liquids, inflames his erotic sensibility to the level of hungry obsession, to hold the open yoni, to know it, to pleasure it ad infinitum. Andrés is safe in the bed of Mila, and can allow these extremes to run real.

M: "Don't stop, ever."

A: "I'm weeping inside that you let me touch you like this."

M: "Don't stop. And don't cry like a girl."

A: "This is the juice of your kundalini."

M: "Don't stop and don't tell me what that word means."

In the midst of the sacred, they laugh with nonsensical happiness.

Gradually Mila's body has rotated so she is nearly flat on her back. She continues to hold herself open. His hand is in perfect position to touch, to enter with fingers, to excite. Also, they can look each other in the eyes now.

They do so while he finds the increasingly clear path to her coming.

M: "Touch me."

A: "My hand loves you."

M: "Oh fuck, touch me."

A: "Right in the wide open girl."

M: "Oh fuck oh fuck oh fuck..."

She reaches the end of words. Her breath catches in her chest. Her eyes grow huge with the vision of where he is taking her with his smart arrogant hand. She ascends, coasting up in a violent, silenced rocket to the void. Her voice bursts open at the top and her crash landing is loud, flooded, and shakes the bed like a berserk earthquake.

Minutes float by. Mila drifts down. He has withdrawn his hand. She has now crossed both her arms behind her knees and pulled herself into the bent-in-half posture he loves so much. Andrés knows there is clenching and squeezing going on in between.

M: "Please let me ask to be fucked."

A: "No."

M: "I'll beg if you want me to."

A: "No."

M: "Our very first time, you let me beg. You let me beg to be fucked."

A: "You weren't surrendered to me then. You didn't ask. You just started begging, like it was your right to beg, a right you don't have at this moment."

She rotates onto her belly, arches her back, pulls knees up under, bottom rising high. This gesture, the blatant offering in violation of the rules, sends him white-hot behind the eyes.

M: "Please fuck me."

Andrés moves behind.

M: "Please."

A: "Let me see. Show me."

M: "Please Andrés, for the love of God, please fuck me."

Thighs open. She tilts up even more and pulls lips apart with shining fingers. His urge leaps high and ripe. The

entry, strong. Right inside. Her plaintive, helpless moan:
M: "Oh ..."

chapter 28
standing in a moment
Tuesday, June 10, 2014
2:30 a.m.

From The White Sky: **After a brutal fight ... making up ...**

Andrés backs away from her body completely.
A: "Put your hands behind your back."
She does this gracefully, proudly. He moves in on her, pressing her into the corner. The difference in size and weight between them incites the power exchange.
A: "Your hands are tied. I don't need to hold them with mine. Can you get loose?"
M: "No," she said, twisting her shoulders. "Tight."
A: "Hold your head up. Expose your neck."
Mila obeys, with a shake of the head to urge her hair back over her shoulder, turning and tilting, then struggling again to see if she can get hands free. She cannot. Andrés begins a relentless traverse of her neck with his wet mouth, her head staying up, forced into his demands by invisible bindings. His weight presses, his hands roam her torso.
A: "Say 'time in'."
Two more kisses below her jaw provoke hot sighs from her throat.
M: "No."
A: "Say it."
When she remains silent, he stops kissing. She spins to face him. He looks into her large brown eyes. Strength

and confidence shine out. Her face is set in an expression of quiet power. He is starkly aware that they are standing in a moment when she has ascended to a new height, the meaning of which it is so certain it thrills: Mila is a magnificent woman.

M: "My consent is given at all times, Andrés. I trust you. I don't want to say "time in" anymore. I'll say the safe word if I need it. I am permanently surrendered to you." She throws off her constraints. An invitation to start fresh.

Andrés shakes to the root. The magnificent woman has said this. All previous appraisals of his possession of her suddenly are as nothing, compared to the depth of ownership now given.

M: "Take me," Mila whispers.

Andrés lifts Mila in his arms and carries her to the bed. This has become a signature move for them.

M: "Every time you carry me like this, my heart breaks open and I get wet."

Andrés stands rock solid at the foot of their bed. She has said this thing draped across his arms with her hands around his neck and head against his chest. It could have been a pose found in the dreams of a romance-crazy teenage girl ... except this particular woman – this magnificent woman – is a valiant warrior fresh from battle.

A: "I will drink the wet now. That will heal your broken heart."

He lowers her into the bed. The permanent, wordless consent shines from her eyes. In his actions to follow, he must swim in much more than the sexual sea. She is ashore on the solid earth, yet the salt water is found flowing between her thighs. He takes all on his tongue.

Only their two serene souls can replenish.

chapter 29

his match

Thursday, June 12, 2014
10:30 p.m.

From The White Sky: **She walks with a new seriousness
through the beach house. Whatever clung to her shoulders
does not appear to weigh her down, only to make Mila look
taller. She grasps the doorknob of Andrés' room with
conviction as never before. Her lover awaits inside.**

They rest in his bed.

M: "In the afterglow."

A: "That's what this is?"

M: "Yes. A ridiculous word, I guess, you'd mock it ...
except if you are in it. Because the sex was good."

His head lies on her belly. His right hand rests over the
Cesarean scar. As gratifying as fast-sex-after-two-days-
apart was, Andrés assumes Mila would like more.

He would like more.

A: "I'm going to ask instead of telling now."

M: "How come?"

A: "I like telling you what to do. But if I always initiate
and then control, I'll never get to see your drives."

M: "Really."

A: "Correct."

M: "Took you a while to figure that out."

A: "Can you describe them? Your drives? What you'd
really like?"

M: "I refuse to do that."

A: "What if I start ordering you to run our sex life? For a
week. Based on your libido."

M: "I will get pouty without my Patagonian cowboy

riding me down on his horse from nowhere."

A: "Do you expect me to initiate sex forever?"

M: "Yes."

Andrés snorts. He moves his hand over her abdomen and thighs.

A: "I don't even know if your hot days are coming and going, because you've never said no. You haven't said your safe word in a week."

M: "So I might be faking?"

He sits up abruptly.

A: "No!"

M: "Sorry. I take it back."

A: "Not faking, but you might be giving in to me sometimes even if you are not in the mood, out of generosity. Are you?"

M: "No man wants to find out we're just going along for the ride sometimes."

A: "I do."

Their eyes duel. There is no cruelty.

A: "I have to say something, Mila. It's risky, but I have to. It's without accusation, but I have to."

M: "Say it."

A: "Don't ever fake orgasm with me, Mila."

M: "I have not and I will not and I am not mad you said that."

A: "I will never say that to you again. Never. But it stands forever. Don't ever."

M: "Okay, Patagonia."

A: "I'm going to give you orders now."

M: "Okay."

A: "You have to tell me your libido temperature for the next ten minutes."

M: "Crap."

A: "Do what I say."

Mila nods slowly.

A: "Tell me what's left of that orgasm."

He continues to caress her thighs and belly. She remains flat on her back.

M: "My muscles are at peace. There's no squeezing going on. They feel soft, all inside my vagina, around my clit. Soft and almost disappeared."

A: "Is my hand making you relax more or heat up?"

M: "Relax."

A: "So, right at this very second, your desire is not growing?"

M: "No. I'm in the afterglow and I like it."

A: "What about deeper?"

M: "The orgasm released a lot. My lower back, in the muscles of my pelvis and around my anus. All buttery and released."

A: "Would you say more than usual or usual?"

She does not answer the question, distracted by an upheaval of bliss.

M: "Oh God, I love to come. I love to feel creamy after, when the contractions end. Make me come like this all the time. I love sex. I love sex, Andrés. To come with your cock slamming into me. Then to float in the cream."

A: "Would you say butterier and softer than usual or usual?"

M: "A little more. Everything was bound up, waiting for you for two days, waiting while knowing you'd be returning."

A: "Really."

M: "Yes. I knew it was okay to let it build up. I channeled it into work."

A: "You can do that?"

M: "Yes."

A: "So because you let it build up, the release is deeper than usual right now?"

M: "Yes."

Their eyes grow more intense because they both see the next question coming.

A: "You didn't masturbate?"

M: "No."

A: "Neither did I."

M: "So, forty-eight hours of you, splashing around

inside my vagina right now."

A: "Yes."

She shows hunger in her eyes and quiets her voice to a whisper. She brushes her next words onto his rugged face as if painting with her juices.

M: "I love to come. To be well fucked."

A: "Oh."

M: "I love it, Andrés. Fuck me and love me and eat me and make me come."

Mila performs a gesture, his favorite thing. She folds deeply at the waist and brings her knees up to her chest, then straightens her legs. Her two feet aim together over her left shoulder. She does it without assistance from her hands. The movement pulls her bottom up and presents the pressed-together puffed lips of her outer sexual organs very explicitly. It is erotic.

M: "Forty-eight hours of you, inside my vagina right now. Inside here."

A: "Yes."

M: "I feel the slipperiness inside."

A: "It's a lot?"

M: "Some may have gone through my cervix into my womb."

Andrés closes his eyes. He has met his match in sexual imagination. In her frank directness of speaking when at peace – and her berserk screaming when coming – Mila Vovk is his match. He opens his eyes and lets them meet hers.

A: "In our imagination, if we were young and in love and mating, would you let it find its way all the way up?"

M: "No more babies for me, Andrés. My eggs are gone. But you can impregnate me every time in your imagination if you wish."

Andrés' eyes fill. He is not sobbing, only leaking. His head does not move. Neither does his woman, her hands flat on the bed, her legs straight, extended all the way up high to her shoulder. She calmly watches his tears.

M: "When my vagina and womb contract because of

coming, they splash your seed around. They dip the cervix in it. To get the sperms swimming into my womb to make me pregnant."

A: "Fuck."

M: "Do you have another release rising?"

A: "Yes. Look how hard I am."

M: "There's s a hot spot now. In my pelvis. Ignore it. Open my legs and put your cock in me. Splash me again. Whether I come again or not. I want the seed."

Andrés does not stop his tears. He shudders as his hands take control of her legs to carefully spread them. Mila closes her eyes and accepts the penetration with an exquisite long sigh. His strokes seek only one thing, and reach it after beautiful long thrusting and urging, the bursting of what little ejaculate remains, aimed at the round pink organ inside with, at its center, the opening, tenderly parted, offered.

chapter 30

the water of that place

Friday, June 13, 2014
9:30 p.m.

From The White Sky: **With a violent rush, the door swings open. A powerful hand grabs her by the wrist and pulls her inside. The door slams shut, heedless of any need for quiet. From the corridor could be heard the sound of something heavy thumped up against the door and the escape of a high-pitched squeal of fright and delight.**

Andrés is at the top of his power. Mila receives his gorgeous rage in it. Her outburst when slammed against the door by his naked body reverberates in the room. She cries out again when he rudely grasps her wrists and pins them high above her head. No verbal order needed – she is bound tight and stretched. He roams her defenseless body with both hands, greedy, moving fast with urgency. His mouth follows. As never before, his hunger explodes.

A: "The entire night, all those people ... all I wanted was the taste of you in my mouth. It has driven me mad."

Andrés sinks to his knees. His hands get behind her thighs. His swift intent is unmistakable.

M: "No no no no no."

He takes her weight with the strength of his upper body, bending her at the waist, lifting, thrusting her against the door with legs wide open, pinned by his hands in the crook of her knees. Instantly his mouth engulfs Mila's sex. He shakes it like a starving lion.

M: "Oh my fucking God ..."

She turns her screaming inward, which would otherwise

pierce the ceiling of their small bedroom and electrify the
sleeping guests and the party room above. Instead, she
fills her heaving chest with fire-power, lets it rattle her
breath and racing heart. Mila's head tilts upward, eyelids
and lashes wet with the flush of it. She reaches her hands
higher up the door and arches her back, as if offering her
breasts with brazen intent, wishing his mouth would suck
them too.

M: "Eat me, oh my fucking God, eat me."

As with a kiss on a girl fully surrendered in mouth and
throat, Andrés invades her lower mouth like a victor. She
is wide open. No resistance. The pink flesh slithers under
his tongue, against the undersides of his lips. The scent
and taste of woman mainlines directly into his tissues. He
sinks deeper. The descent into cunt unleashes the
unspeakable primal, the taste of fertility that birthed the
first living thing, filling it with remorseless urging.

He never ceases his quest until the water of that place,
stinging with salt, floods his mouth. He drinks it all.

chapter 31

nothing under

Sunday, June 15, 2014
11:30 p.m.

From The White Sky: the party, Mila circles toward
Andrés sitting in the welcoming chair/sofa. Swaying in her
party dress to flirt, she soon slips onto his lap. She takes the
camera from his hands and sets it gently on the floor.
   "Is it a sacrilege to have a make-out party after stern
words from your mentor?" Mila asks.
   "Lydia would want us to carry on."
   And that's exactly what they did.

They really like the chair. It is big and soft and they fit it
perfectly, she draped over him, arms around his neck,
head tilted and offered. Not a creature is stirring, just
them. Not a sound, just theirs – the sounds of the tiny
wet intimacies that thrill as kisses incite desire.
   Ten minutes in, Mila pulls off, suppressing a giggle.
   A: "What?"
   M: "Your hand."
   A: "What about it?"
   M: "Did you forget it? You haven't moved it."
   His right hand rests right on her belly. Right on her
abdomen. Right where it should be.
   M: "A girl wants it to move after ten minutes, you
know."
   A: "What does a woman want?"
   M: "A woman can wait longer."
   A: "Are you in a hurry?"
   M: "You kiss like anything. How can your hand be so

patient?"

A: "I want this to go a certain way."

M: "Yeah, but ..."

Perfect happy mischief appears on her face.

A: "You want my hand on you."

A solemn nod.

A: "You have to say it."

M: "Touch me."

A: "Mila."

M: "Touch them."

A: "... petting like teenagers?"

M: "Yeah. My dad's in the next room and he thinks we are watching television."

A: "Ha!"

M: "But really I am hoping you will dare make them bare and touch them."

A: "Do you feel old or young?"

M: "Young. Because an elder died. And we have been around children."

As they talk, the trace-taste of her mouth grows strong, with phantom juice seeming to fall from his lips to spill in their laps. He grieves for every drop. He must kiss them back together so no liquids are lost – real or dreamed. He is about to, feels the wonderful ache of lips reaching for lips, but then – the rich yearning to take command floods in. He lets it overwhelm all, dimming their mutuality. The unstoppable lust *to take* runs right up his spine.

A: "Unbutton."

Her hand jumps to obey.

A: "Not fast."

Mila can do it with one hand, her left. Her right arm stays around his neck. With delicacy she visits each button of the black blouse from top to bottom until all are snapped open. The garment parts slightly. She wears nothing under.

Andrés holds her eyes with his and slides his hand under the silk, resting it below her navel. It inches up. A clenching of the muscles in her core. He stops. She relaxes. He continues. She flinches again. He stops. This ballet requires two more such pauses. Andrés will not move his hand until he feels absolute surrender. His fingers, finally, rest on the under-curve.

A: "Say it."

M: "Touch my breasts."

She affords the smile of a coquette and a subtle arcing of the torso. Andrés enters a trance. He burns to bend her over the chair and ravage her deep. He is in charge. She would have to comply, leaving her lonely breasts untouched. Gradually making that rage recede, his expressive hand opens to fit itself to her shape. He cups under. He turns his wrist to brush the back of his hand against. He lets a nipple slip between two fingers. All unseen caresses, the touching under the black silk blouse.

He stops. It is Mila and Andrés looking deep in each other's eyes while his hand holds her breast. Just that.

M: "There it is again."

A: "What?"

M: "Just a body part of a woman. In the light of day and the run of a lifetime just my ordinary body parts."

A: "But in the light of lovers?"

M: "Yes."

A: "Lovely."

M: "Yes."

Andrés resumes caressing. He shifts from one to the other. Mila coos her agreement with every move. The very act of forming his fingers into the shape of her – this itself brings fire.

M: "Touch them."

A: "Move your body against my hand."

He holds his hand steady while Mila rotates and arcs her torso into it. She hisses in breaths through lips tight with pleasure.

Andrés notices her blouse is fastened at the wrist by cufflinks. This sparks instant action. He sits up straight, which disturbs their positions. His hands go under her shirt from the hem and slide up to the shoulders.

Gathering it, twisting it tight, it pulls her hands together behind her neck. Her back is bent and her beautiful bare breasts tilt prominently forward. He has uncovered them like exposing ripe fruits to the morning.

Mila has made no sound of protest, no hint of resistance, only let the smile of the willing captive alight on her lips.

A: "Stand up."

In a moment, Andrés is walking behind the girl with the bare feet, the swirly skirt, the naked torso, with hands bound behind by twisted black silk. They move slowly through the great room, past the dining table, into the kitchen.

A: "I'm leading you off into captivity."

M: "Is the food any good?"

A: "You get gruel. I get peaches and cream."

M: "Fuck, Andrés ..."

A: "Yeah, that was a good one."

She tries to stop the march and spin around. He grabs the twisted blouse at the juncture of her hands to prevent it. His open mouth fits over her shoulder and finds her neck, sliding along as if searching for the spot to sink his teeth. His hand circles around and caresses her breasts. It is heartbreaking how unprotected they are.

M: "You're making me wet."

Andrés pushes her forward. They stumble out of the kitchen. Along the corridor they pass Leo's room, its door half open. They can't help peeking in.

M: "Nope."

A: "Nope."

But at the back of the house, where the corridor turns left, the door to Kaarin's room is shut tight. Instinctively, they both slow and quiet their steps. Andrés' urges her forward, pushing her head up against the door with her ear on it, gripping the binding tight so she can't move. Mila attempts to control her excited breathing. All grows quiet.

After a moment, he releases her head and she looks in his

eyes. She whispers.

M: "Nothing."

Ten steps along, he stops them at his door. He pulls her body against his from behind.

A: "I'd have made you listen, if a girl were crying out behind that door."

She nods.

A: "I'd have made you tell me what her screams meant, what you visualized her doing. What position you think she was in."

M: "It makes me furious when you force my head against a door like that, or tape it to the wall. What the hell do you think you're doing?"

A: "You love it."

She is breathing fast. Her shoulders rotate as if to ward off two violations, his infuriating grip on her body and his knowing her pleasures in sex. Finally, she quiets and answers.

M: "I love it."

A: "What else. I'll let you say one more thing."

M: "My breasts are burning from your touch. I have taught you how to know by touch."

Andrés spins her around, forcing her shoulder blades and her bound hands against the door. His right hand moves over her heart, the forearm nestling between and pressing against. Holding her eyes with his, he whispers.

A: "I already knew how."

M: "No, you didn't."

A: "I know how to touch a woman."

M: "But now you know how to make her burn."

A: "You're not wearing anything under this skirt, are you?"

M: "No. After all the dancing and twirling, I went in the bathroom and took them off."

Andrés' left hand reaches down to gather the hem of the garment. His right keeps her pinned against the door. With fear in her eyes, Mila turns to look down the corridor.

M: "We could get caught."

A: "I want you exposed."

M: "Not here."

His hand has reached the inside of her thigh, high up. He feels her trying to block – and stay surrendered – at the same time. That is exciting.

A: "Exposed. Right here. Anyone could come along."

M: "No. Please, no."

A: "There is no way to escape. I'll only let you cover yourself after I hear you come. Right here in the hall."

M: "Oh my God."

His hand goes home. It affords no mercy. Never before has he felt so much panic between her legs. He senses Mila panicking over the predicament he has put on her, then feels her release all barriers. So she can obey.

She melts.

A: "There."

M: "Oh my God."

A: "There, now you are wide open."

Mila cannot speak. She becomes a panting, moaning creature, a beautiful woman unprotected against herself. His hand cannot be stopped. Parts of it enter her body, touching her clitoris, the inside part of it and the glans. It loves her so much she becomes queasy inside, thrashing angrily against it, flinging the start of her orgasm against the rude fingers. Mila's scream is about to reverberate down the corridor. Andrés takes his right hand from her breast and clamps it over her mouth. This act of mercy does not help – it only proves his power.

Never again will she say Andrés' hands do not *know*. The hand controlling her mouth and the one inflaming her sex, creamed with her juices ...

They know.

They burn.

grasps the hem of her shirt

Monday, June 16, 2014
1:30 p.m.

From The White Sky: **Mila and Andrés are focused on a project at the huge family table in the beach house, which has emptied except for their two friends who are in a remote part of the house. Mila is mistaken when she says she and Andrés must stick with the work.**

"We can't be fooling around."
He says: "Yes we can!"

Before Mila can react, Andrés vaults onto the table, grabs her around the waist, and pulls her onto its sturdy surface. She squeals.

M: "Andrés! They'll hear us."

A: "So?"

Then they are laughing, tussling, yanking off each other's clothes. She is successful -- he is naked. He gets her pants off, but cannot finish stripping her. She pins his arms against the table. He breaks her grip and wrestles himself on top.

M: "Bastard."

A: "I'm not letting you on top."

They struggle madly. Wrapping legs around his waist gives her enough leverage to tip him over by throwing her hips left and right. Each tussle to get back in control. In a moment of frustration, they freeze.

A: "Not on the sacred family table."

Mila breaks free and jumps off. Andrés slides off. She
stands six feet away with index finger raised as a warning.
The finger gets emphatic.

M: "Don't."

A: "I can, I will, you can't stop me."

M: "Don't."

He does not charge. It releases her dramatic persona.
Mila turns her back on him, with the warning hand
thrust behind, palm up, solid.

M: "Mind the hand."

A melodrama.

Andrés snorts with ridicule. He could run right over her
ridiculous stop sign. Mila steps into the great room with
excruciating slowness. Gradually the hand descends, but
she keeps an eye on him over her shoulder. Andrés
follows, just out of striking distance. Mila ends her
procession in the middle of the room, turning and
stopping next to their favorite oversized chair with its
black velvet fabric.

M: "This is our make-out chair."

A: "Yes."

M: "We have never been naked in it."

A: "No."

M: "Never engaged in sexual intercourse in it."

A: "Never." He smiles at her silly words.

Mila crosses her arms, grasps the hem of her shirt, and
pulls it straight up over her torso, through her hair and
off, tossing it in an arc toward Andrés. It falls at his feet.

M: "Until now."

The hand rises in warning again. Mila sits on the right
arm-rest of the giant chair. Her feet dangle towards the
floor. She looks small and wonderful.

M: "Somehow, you got a woman naked again."

A: "Yes."

M: "You should always have a girl around, naked and
ready. Do you want women or girls?"

A: "The woman who gives her carnal body with the
sweetness of a happy girl."

M: "The happy girl is in my heart, loving you."

Mila spins into the chair and leans forward toward the opposite arm rest. Breasts drop as torso falls. She arches her back, causing her bottom to rise, to round up, to offer.

She turns her head to look over her shoulder, aiming right between his eyes.

M: "The woman is right here."

chapter 33

without another
word

Monday, June 16, 2014
8:30 p.m.

From The White Sky: **They venture outside to make love on a deck in the yard of the beach house. The deck is a viewing platform for a large boulder. First, she invokes one of his former lovers ...**

M: "Teach me something Pari taught you."

A: "Hunh?"

Andrés and Mila sit on the edge of the deck, he completely naked, she wearing a ludicrously long cotton nightgown with a fancy embroidered collar around the neck, tight over the torso, falling straight down to the ground from the hips, another treasure from the Boston trip. It requires her hands gathering it up when she walks. She insisted on donning this ironic garment – her fourth outfit of the day – before joining him *for joining* on the deck. They savor the deliberate reversal of their she-nude-he-not paradigm. If not for their satisfying date on the velvet chair earlier, they would not be hesitating. They would be in impetuous conjugation.

M: "Teach me something Pari taught you. Some deep Hindu mystery about sex."

A: "I can't remember what I told you about her and sex."

M: "She doesn't want either of you to fall in love, but she'll take all the Andrés she can get in the ... dating bed."

A: "Okay."

M: "But you also said she knows secret wisdom about

both love and sex."

A: "This is what you want to talk about?"

M: "Does that frighten you?"

A: "Hmm."

M: "Wait, let's phone her. I know you've got her India number on your phone. Put her on speaker and I'll ask her."

A: "Whoa. No, Mila."

M: "It'll be sexy, your ex and your *now*, having girl-talk about your penis while you listen."

A: "Oh for crying out loud."

M: "Is that phrase even a thing in Spanish?"

A: "No. I got it from Pari, who got it from her English-guy-Oxford-ex before Pari got me. I think he got it from an undergrad feminist from New Jersey. For crying out loud."

M: "Very funny."

They pause, eyeing each other, legs dangling, the nearly-dusk sun attempting to get behind the boulder. Andrés lets her stew for a good long minute before giving in.

A: "Okay."

M: "Yea! Will it get me nirvana orgasms?"

He ignores her silliness. Something serious just occurred to him.

A: "Mila?"

M: "Yes?"

A: "I'll tell you the one that was supposed to be about sex, but I think it crosses over."

M: "Pari almost fell in love with you on it?"

A: "Yes."

M: "What is it?"

A: "Womb-space."

Mila's legs stop dangling. She does not move a muscle. She holds his gaze carefully.

M: "Womb-space?"

A: "Yes."

M: "Wait. Don't tell me. Don't say anything."

Mila eases off the deck. She is moving slowly. She walks

carefully into the back of the dell. She lifts the gown only enough to avoid tripping, letting it trail behind on the new grass. She turns and strolls back, passing within six feet of Andrés. It's like watching the deliberation of a queen. She stops near the mouth of the dell and turns her eyes on him.

M: "Womb-space?"

A: "Yes."

Then, Mila disappears. She has turned and walked to the boulder and behind it. The sun has not set below the horizon, but it has succeeded in descending behind the ice-age rock, casting shadows on the deck. Andrés stands up, seeing if the rock will shade his eyes, and it does. There is little sound, not the muted suggestion of waves on the shore, not the flutter of birds. There is no breeze. He is naked, waiting in a temple for the celebrant.

Mila emerges from the other side of the boulder. Her face might be solemn, but also glinting with delight. He has come to know she can inhabit both houses at the same time. She walks to the edge of the deck and elevates her hand to him. He helps her climb on. With simplicity, Mila unbuttons the gown down its bodice. Her shoulders shiver to make the garment ease off and down. She is soon naked.

M: "Teach me."

Andrés kneels by her side. His right hand settles on her abdomen. Mila places her hand on his shoulder.

A: "No. Leave your hands at your side."

When she removes her hand, Andrés reinforces:

A: "Just let me touch. Any touch I need to make."

M: "Okay."

His hand slips down. His fingers point straight back up her body, the heel stopping just above the top of her sex lips. Most of the scar from Mila's Caesarean section disappears under his palm.

A: "Your womb is here. Your uterus."

M: "Yes."

A: "It's an ordinary body part. Functional. Flesh and

organs."

M: "Yes."

A: "Even if all we are is the organic computer, the mechanical automation of a node of life, still this particular body part is amazing."

M: "Yes."

A: "But if we choose a purpose, activate our will, then everything takes on value. The act of valuing ourselves can ... it should ... rise to the level of metaphor, actually a myth, but a true myth."

M: "That is the soul, Andrés."

He orders Mila to kneel down next to him. His hand remains over her uterus, but swivels laterally.

A: "So, the idea of womb-space is to allow the female principle to gather in the womb, and then the person, the woman, can tap into this power. It is the power to give birth to life, after all."

M: "So, Pari did this?"

A: "She told me she used to practice visualizing the womb-space, breathing into it, drawing in all the visions of millions of birthings of all the billions of women, and also all the orgasms she had had, investing power there. Then when she went forward into the world, she was always 'leading with the womb.' That's what she called it."

M: "Well, now I really want to phone her. No kidding. Did she have sex with you ... leading with the womb?"

A: "Yes."

M: "And that's when she nearly fell in love with you."

A: "Yes."

M: "Because you were the only man who ever understood it and didn't reject it. She told you what was going on with her womb, the only man she ever told?"

A: "Yes."

M: "This is Tantric."

A: "I think so. I don't know. I have an 'expanded Andrés theory' for it."

M: "You do?"

A: "Yes. Tell me about you 'finding the sweet spot'."

Mila goes shy. She looks away from his eyes. She rotates her body down to the mattress they have placed on the deck. Face down. His hand is no longer on her body.

M: "It's the same thing, isn't it? You were teaching me how to find it."

A: "Well, similar. My theory is that it's more than the womb. It's the total of the female organs: the uterus, the ovaries, the tubes, the vagina, the lips and the clitoris. All of it. But more, it's the entire energy field around it all."

M: "Andrés, you think we can call it ... that 'C' word we like."

A: "Yes."

M: "Don't. Don't say it. It might have been the right word once, but it's destroyed.

A: "Yes. It's a shame. Let's use the word 'yoni'."

There is another moment of silence. Andrés waits, but then cannot.

A: "Why won't you look at me?"

Mila turns over on her back.

M: "Put your hand on my womb."

His hand slips into place. Andrés is filled with warmth from her asking for it and allowing it. His hand on her womb.

M: "I'm not believing in you again."

A: "This is real."

M: "No. Men are not like this. You are not for real."

A: "I'm just a guy who has loved women since I was born. I love them. I told you I did. You didn't realize I meant it. You were blind enough to pick me for your model and now your mind is blown."

M: "Yes."

A: "I don't know what Tantra is all about, Mila. I didn't study it. I just know that this energy flows at the root of a woman. I've been in bed with it flowing, even when some of them did not feel it themselves. That's all. I connected up with Pari, who knew some things."

M: "Move your hand down and touch me. Put your

fingers inside me."

A: "No."

M: "Please."

A: "Finding your sweet spot, is it a real thing? Not fake?"

Mila requires several deep breaths before answering. She allows Andrés to look in her eyes, finally, when she responds.

M: "Yes. Several times now, when you were not around, I looked for it on our bed in the studio."

A: "You did?"

M: "Yes. I practiced finding it."

Andrés waits.

M: "I felt it. With you not in the bed, I lost my shyness. I opened my legs. I let it happen. I rotated my hips with my legs moving, to find it. My hands were flat on the bed. Andrés, it's real. There is something. I found it, the place where I'm innocent and naked and free. Completely exposed as a woman. My pelvis started shaking. My lower back, then the rest of me. Then the shaking stopped and I was ... somewhere. Time was gone. Then suddenly, I knew what to do. My hand moved in between. I just touched lightly. My fingers went inside."

Mila still permits his eyes looking into hers. Andrés can feel her lower body quivering under his hand.

"It was an orgasm. I don't know how long it lasted. It was so deep I could not scream. Or cry. It went in waves. When it ended, I lowered my legs. Everything was wet. Eventually I returned to reality. I cried for about an hour."

She has not taken her gaze away. Mila is sad and peaceful and full of gladness all at the same time. But she is crying.

Andrés reclines beside her and takes her in his arms. He pulls the cotton nightgown over them to keep their warmth close.

M: "Are you my guru?"

A: "I'm just your lover."

They fall asleep without another word.

chapter 34

her wide-open erotic heart

Monday, June 16, 2014
9:50 p.m.

From The White Sky: Up against a gigantic boulder on the property ... Mila seeks to be bound for sex ...

Andrés holds Mila around the waist off the ground. She has been struggling, now has gone limp. He folds her over his shoulder. Like a sack of something. Andrés is indecisive for a second. What to do with the sack?

A: "Hell, nothing here to tie you down with."

M: "Put me down for a second."

Andrés complies. Mila stands right in front of him, the boulder two feet behind. It is night now, but they can see because of an LED lantern on the ground ten feet away. She puts her arms around his neck.

M: "Use pretend ropes. Nail imaginary rings into the rock and use the ropes to tie me up. I can't get loose from them any easier than real ones."

Now she whispers so quietly he can barely hear her imploring voice.

M: "Fuck me against the rock, Andrés. Tie me up. Then fuck me against the rock."

What other salacious things will Mila say? She is existential and risky.

M: "In a few seconds, I'll have your cock in me. In my vagina."

A: "Yes."

M: "That is so good, my cowboy ... standing here wide

awake ... looking at you ... knowing it. In a few seconds your body will be inside mine."

A: "Yes."

With all the beauty of her wide-open erotic heart, womb forward, the surrendered girl lets loose her whispered plea.

M: "Fuck me."

It takes two seconds to tie Mila to the rock. Her arms, high up. He only ties down one foot, to a stake in the ground. The other leg he grabs behind the thigh. It is this he will use to control her pelvis and the wet between her legs. He yanks the thigh up, spreading her. His raging prick thrusts fast and far in, in the girl, in the woman, in the heart of what he loves and takes.

A: "Cock forward."

chapter 35

screaming, moaning, swearing

Tuesday, June 17, 2014
5:30 a.m.

From The White Sky: Back in New York, they fall asleep early ... Mila and Andrés do not stir for hours. The swirl of Manhattan all around, their own journey back to the island of their love affair pending on awakening ... nothing shakes the depth of their sleep.

Until the last hour of dark.

Andrés wakes her near the end of the night. They touch gently, kiss, nuzzle, and sigh. Both wake up fully. They take turns in the bathroom and return to bed.

A: "Cross your wrists."

Mila smiles her captured-happiness smile. She is lying on her back, and the command does not include turning over to be bound behind, so she presents her overlapped wrists in front. He opens his hands as if showing her something.

A: "These are fine black velvet ribbons. I'm tying them around, making a bow. You're being bound tight."

Andrés makes an abstracted gesture of tying her up. She makes a convincing effort to wiggle free.

M: "They are so tight. I'll never get them undone."

A: "Never. You are bound forever."

Her breathing accelerates on the word 'forever.' It feels like real panic.

A: "Settle down. Settle down."

Dark looks. More heaving breaths and wrenching at the ribbons. Andrés waits her out. It takes a minute for the bindings to subdue her rebellion. When resigned, she turns her head to the wall.

A: "Mila."

No response.

A: "Look at me."

Her head turns. He gets a shock. Mila is smiling with wet eyes. She breaks into laughter. She separates her hands and gestures with them – as unbound -- to the ceiling.

M: "Whoops."

A: "Oh ..."

M: "This game is so ridiculous I can barely stand it. I'm up on a mountain with my arms free and wide open to the sky, calling down the forces that put art in my hands. I own the mountain. The art gods gave it to me. 'It's only right,' they said. I can feel it in my feet, it's my mountain. There is nothing below me, except maybe far away near the horizon someone calling me. It's faint."

Andrés puts everything on hold to take in this poem. Mila lowers her arms and re-crosses her wrists, making one quick jerk as if trying to break free, then rests her hands over her chest. Incredulity and laughter infuse every word she speaks.

M: "I am so free. But something's tangled around my hands again. Darn."

A: "Mila, you're not submissive."

Mila's smile broadens. She shakes her head.

M: "No, my wild gaucho, not even a drop of it in my blood. I am so free."

He feels the distinctive shudder in the bed that tells him Mila is contracting the muscles in her pelvis, heating the core of sex. He sees the mounting arousal in her eyes.

A: "Then why can't you escape the ribbons around your wrists?"

M: "The happiness of being free in my center, but pretending I am a captive – this makes me melt. That sounds poetic, but it's very real. I can feel everything melting. Right. Between. My. Legs."

A: "Wow."

M: "I adore being bound."

She continues squirming on the bed.

M: "Melting. Just ... so ... wet."

He watches her make three more rotations of her pelvis.

M: "But it's so sad: I'm bound. I can't put my fingers there. I want to come and I can't with these stupid ribbons."

A: "We've known it was a game all along. That you are not submissive."

M: "But knowing I'm not makes it a lot more exciting."

A: "I'm in love with the free girl."

M: "Oh ... Oh. That feels good, like the lingam just hit the right spot."

They laugh and tease with eyes. Then hers gradually squint down. She lifts her crossed wrists to him.

M: "The ribbons are too tight. They are burning me. Andrés, please, they hurt."

He shifts his position and brings both hands to her wrists.

M: "Please, Andrés."

A: "I am not taking the loose ends in my fingers. I'm holding the bows. I have a rage inside too. You think you are free?"

M: "Oh no."

A: "I'm not going to loosen them. I'm going to tug them tight, really tight."

M: "Oh no, oh God. Wait. Wait. Wait."

Mila's eyes grow large, openly staring at the audacity and surety in his face. She gathers her strength, pulling in a giant breath, letting it out. Emptying.

A: "Did you just go 'womb forward'?"

M: "That's right, Master."

Andrés pulls the bows. Mila moans from the belly as the ribbons bite deep. She screams at him, eyes hot with passion.

M: "You are too cruel in my bed."

His right hand slips between her thighs, pushing them apart. His fingers sink into the melted sex. She bellows with pleasure. Mila's lower body clinches and the bed shakes once, one wooden leg of it grating on the floor. She arches high off the bed and freezes, her voice jammed in her throat. His hand does not stop its stirring of the liquids, the slushing of her tissues clearly audible.

The fingers moving in her wide open soaked sex do terrible damage. Then suddenly, she slams back down, screaming, moaning, and swearing.

His hand remains in place, stroking her into rolling waves, diminishing yet delicious, until she shifts her hips and brings her thighs together. That body language – the 'close down' – is prior communication: 'thank you forever you fantastic man but let me coast now.' Andrés removes his hand and watches through to the end. Amazingly, her hands remain on her chest, crossing at the wrists. She has certainly been pressing her breasts nicely with them. Her legs quiver, and her pelvis jerks several times.

They lay in the bed for many minutes without a word, while her breathing slows. Every once in a while Mila squeezes her thighs together and contracts the muscles in her pelvis, to suck in deliciousness for the tissues drained by orgasm. Their eyes meet, sometimes, or drift apart at peace. A persistent call in his lower body throbs.

A: "I can't believe how fast that was."

M: "I'm keyed up. Hyper-sensitive. And your hand is very talented ... about the Yoni. It belongs in the Yoni, Andrés. You've got me in a state. Pulling the ribbons tight when I asked you to cut them sent me flying."

Andrés wants to touch again. It is a pure impulse. He must, even if his penetration urge is screaming from deep in his pelvis. His eyes hold hers steady. His hand finds its way to the delta, from below her thigh. The yielding, once again she lets the hand – she lets it. It eases her legs apart. With confidence the fingers separate swollen lips and slip inside.

A: "My hand belongs here."

Mila nods, smiling quietly with hooded eyelids, drunk

on the dopamine of release turning into new heat.

Andrés withdraws the hand, lifting it to his face. He imparts the girl-juice to his lips.

M: "Unbelievable. You like the taste?"

A: "Yes. I love it."

M: "I'll never want you to stop drinking me."

A: "I always want your juice in my mouth."

Mila's laugh gurgles up.

M: "We are ridiculously oral."

A: "It is ridiculous."

M: "When we're not doing it, we're talking about it. Everything is oral with these two."

A: "We only talk about it to stir us up to do it again."

M: "No. We talk about it for the oral pleasure of talking about it."

A: "We do?"

M: "Yes. It feels good to talk about sex. It's oral. I feel good right now."

A: "So we are having oral sex at this very instant?"

M: "Yes."

They laugh at their silliness together, rolling in the bed. Then Mila simmers to a stop.

M: "Andrés."

A: "What?"

M: "Please."

A: "What?"

M: "Please oral. But don't stop this time. Make me come with your mouth ... but then keep going. With your mouth."

Mila's face is serious, full of risk.

A: "Be careful what you wish for."

M: "I don't want to be careful."

A: "If you ask me for this, will you really let go?"

M: "I'll need to come more than once. I don't know how many times. Until I get to the end of it. Yes, I'll let go. To find out how far it is."

A: "I'm giving you a different little safe word, Mila, a release word, just for now. When you don't want any more, you have to end it. Not me, you. Just say 'Hold me. Hold me.' Otherwise, I will not stop. Seriously. I won't stop even after an hour, unless I hear those words."

She is up to the challenge.

M: "Go into the bathroom and bring back a warm washcloth. I only want you to have the new juice. The fresh."

The little ritual they perform excites. She shifts her eyes from his face to his hands once or twice. Then Mila speaks her carnal wish. The poetry is on her.

M: "We are oral. I have no shame. It is extreme and so what. We crave the taste of each other. It is beautiful. We accept the liquids of each other, drinking them with purity and pleasure. We love them on our lips and tongues. Eat me and drink me until I am done. I'll ask you to hold me, hold me. But then pull me to the side of the bed so my head bends over the edge. I want the other oral. Stroke in my mouth. Take your pleasure there. Come in my mouth."

unleash the girl dance

Wednesday, June 16, 2014
7:00 p.m.

From The White Sky: In her studio, Mila and Andrés pause the sculpting. They face the arrival of a timespan apart … days, maybe weeks.

Andrés is naked. She makes him swivel the couch until it faces the work area. She makes him assume a reclining pose on it. She heats him by sitting on the floor, still in artist work clothes, caressing his upper body while offering verbal eroticisms and kisses full of intent.

A: "Is this the 'one person nude while the other is not' thing again?"

M: "Yes."

A: "What do you want?"

M: "To know you by touch."

A: "My tactile ferryboat undercover sweetheart."

They laugh in surprise, with keenness as the double meaning goes home.

M: "I knew we were lovers the first time I touched your bare skin."

A: "I thought you were all business on the ferry that day."

M: "No."

A: "What do you want to touch now?"

M: "That without possession of which I am sad."

A: "You must *know* that item to be truly a master of the

male torso?"

M: "Yes. The Greeks knew everything about the male body, and sculpted everything."

A: "Yes. Well, they hadn't read the bible yet, didn't realize they were supposed to be ashamed of it."

Mila's left hand roams his torso. It tends down.

M: "Let me be in charge."

A: "Okay."

Mila takes his organ in hand. As sculptor, the touching seeks to know the shape. As lover, she sends tenderness. Blood swells the flesh. It is soon firm and strong. It has become an erection.

M: "Artists make workups. We talked about it, remember? Sketches. Studies. Mockups."

A: "You did a study of my torso before the full size."

M: "Yes."

A: "Oh. Okay, where this is headed?"

She continues to caress, applying a few drops of oil. Her touch remains unhurried. So comfortable is the intimacy, they can speak while arousal soars.

M: "Studies should never be included in an important exhibition."

A: "No?"

M: "There's a film about Camille Claudel – she makes an impression on Rodin with a foot she sculpted as a study. Maybe it's factual, who knows? It was a cool scene."

A: "You hand is not on my foot."

M: "No."

Mila allows a moment to pass with nothing but the flow of his phallus in the palm of her hand. She removes her eyes from it and turns to him.

M: "Take it in your hand. Touch it like I did. This will be a study."

She stands up, watching for a moment to be sure he follows her order. He has seen this same delight in her expression previously, when he once ordered her to watch him self-stroking while she touched herself. Then Mila

marches over to her work area, returning immediately to
the side of the couch, a box of clay in her hands. She
kneels, opens the box, and extracts a rectangular block of
gray clay, cuts off a section with a wire, and thumps it
onto a turntable she pulled from underneath the couch.

A: "Oh."

M: "Yes."

Working while sometimes kneeling, sometimes sitting
on the floor, Mila forms up the rough shape, then
continues to refine. Andrés notices she does not look at
the actual cock very often – nor down at the clay – she
works with eyes closed. The circuit grows stronger – his
hand on himself, her hand on the clay, and the electrified
connection when she opens her eyes to look in his every
so often.

A: "You can do it with eyes closed?"

M: "Oh yes."

A: "Apparently, you know me. From touch."

M: "Yes."

A: "It's erotic."

M: "Watch my hand. Copy my movements."

Mila's hand strokes with care, not moving the clay as
much as confirming the shape. Andrés watches, then
mimics with his hand, stroking in kind. His free left hand
reaches for the bottle of oil and he applies a small stream
on the head, pulling it down onto the shaft with his right
hand, then obediently resumes echoing the speed,
direction, and temper of Mila's.

Now her intention shifts. Both hands touch the clay.
The tips of fingers converge near the top and press,
forming a ridge – the ridge. As she continues to shape this
detail, emotion crashes his erotic heart. Mila knows. Oh,
Mila knows his organ, his penis, his erection. She sculpts
the budding head above the ridge exactly right – he feels
the exactitude as if justice is served. The pads of two of
her fingers push material apart at the center underside to
create a cleft in the ridge. The sureness of this jolts him.
She has effected even the tiny folds flaring off on an angle

at the delta of this sweet defile. Then, with left hand
wrapped around below the ridge, the corner of the nail of
her right index finger makes a tiny indentation at the apex
of the head. It is perfect.

Her hands ease down the shaft, pausing in one spot to
change the shape slightly, a refinement. The hands slow
with the grace of a dancer's diminuendo, resting finally at
the base. Just this quickly, the sculpture is finished, life
size.

The organ of a man, the shape of penetration, the
erection of arousal – Mila has invoked the quintessence of
male sex. She turns her eyes on his. Her words fall into the
fine silence.

M: "I adore your erection."

A: "Oh ..."

M: "It is the lingam."

A: "Lingam?"

M: "I like 'lingam,' and I think that word for it is
sometimes used by those in the know."

A: "There is no human being on earth more in the know
than Mila Vovk."

M: "About this specific item, you mean."

They laugh with eyes bright. Mila's hands do not move
from the base of her new sculpture. Andrés remains
aroused. They revel in the thick eroticism.

M: "Andrés."

A: "What?"

Mila turns serious. Her nostrils flare. Her head nods
forward and she peers at him from under her brown
eyebrows.

M: "Let me."

Andrés nods. Mila rises and runs to the wash basin. Her
hands are soon clean. Her body is soon naked. She steps
away from the pile of clothes and strides back to the
couch. Andrés' hand has never stopped stroking the
proud cock. Mila's hips rotate over and above. His last
gesture as owner: one hand holds the shaft steady while
the other slips between her lips, pulling them apart. When

Mila lets her weight down, the lingam penetrates her body, thrusting deep, pricking open the membrane of their sexy bubble.

Andrés surrenders to Mila. The echo of her asking 'let me' soothes his drive to control, sets it into abeyance. Her hips, her arms, and the toned muscles in her groin unleash the girl dance. She likes to bend at the waist and push off with arms for leverage, so her mouth stays near his. Several times it brushes his and the oral hunger erupts. She grabs a kiss, making sure her breasts press his chest, rubbing with the rocking. They are both voracious and hungry, with open mouths.

He pulls out of the kiss.

A: "Fuck me. Yes. Like that. Like that. Like that."

She stops his words with her mouth on his. The rhythmic rock and roll of her dance tells in the kiss, a pulse that swirls the inside liquids.

He pulls his mouth away again.

A: "I almost came, watching your hands on the clay."

She reaches the swerving stage – her hips perform a twist and side-slip with each engulfment and squeeze. The dance goes urgent. She rides him for long minutes this way, grunting, squealing, laughing. Andrés can only accept the outrageous fuck of a beautiful woman. His contribution, the gorgeous lingam.

Mila's rocking, shaking, convulsing body dances as if no one is watching. Andrés sees the focus in her eyes depart. She is gone. Her mouth utters insane gurgled words, her hands clenched like eagle claws into the couch. She freezes, staring into the void. Then one, two, three elongated jolts, each slower than the next, her voice silent.

A: "One more ..."

The final slamming, screaming, wet collapse ...

M: "Oh oh oh."

A: "All gone, all gone."

He finds himself with a blubbering, quaking woman squirming on his body, impaled on his erection. Her breaths come in heaving sighs. The girl is dripping all over from the hard work of seeking ecstasy. He moves his hands onto her bottom to cup the ripe flesh, moving it in circles, to help her settle the satisfaction deep. He is in no hurry. The sounds and scent of her in the after-grasp of orgasm bring delight. The muscles in his pelvis contract once or twice, urging the cock deeper. His own eruption is not far from the surface. He waits for the perfect sigh from Mila.

A: "Whisper something wild in my ear. Then squeeze me."

Mila slides her slick body up without allowing them to separate below. Her breasts make a trail on his chest.

M: "I could sculpt your lingam with my mouth."

Andrés groans when this image floods his brain and Mila's sex muscles squeeze. He slams his pelvis upward to drive his fat organ deep.

M: "... or with my vagina."

Once, twice, again – the penetration into soaked flesh, with her rippling it around him, and his release explodes.

A: "Oh oh oh oh oh."

The spraying of her insides, and the fine squeal of the girl when she gets the juice.

End
Andrés + Mila

For the full novel in which their sexual encounters are embedded, please read *The White Sky*.
TheWhiteSky.com
JohnCaedan.com

After

M: "I looked at images of Rodin's Danaïd."

A: "You did?"

M: "I sank into your trope for it."

Mila laughs. They lay face up looking through the skylights into the firmament. She laughs at the universe, not at his wit.

M: "Say my trope."

A: "Camille is collapsed on the floor in a pool of water, exhausted and exhilarated from so much loving. Overcome with happiness."

M: "Yes. She was on the way to filling a bathtub for them to bathe together, but she dropped the water jar, spilling it and cracking it. She is limp from lovemaking. From so many orgasms."

A: "I found out the sick truth of the original myth."

M: "Uh-oh."

A: "Condemned to refill a basin with a jar that has holes in the bottom. For all eternity. Pitiful nightmare repetition of a hopeless task. Worse than Sisyphus. It's hell."

M: "Why are they making her do that?"

A: "Forced into marriage by her uncle's threats, then forced to kill her husband by her father's revenge edict."

M: "Yes, that is the myth."

A: "Thank you for destroying it, Mila."

Mila slides out of bed. She is sober. Andrés watches her move, stop, sigh, and then stand perfectly still for nearly a minute. An early summer breeze flows through the studio from the screen door facing Lagoon Pond.

M: "When I told my mother Camille was exulting from sex, I didn't actually mean it. I said it to insult my mother good. Like a punch in the face."

A: "Now?"

Mila returns to the bedside. She kneels on the floor and brings her lips close to his.

M: "Now it is true.

August Rodin - Danaïd

Camille Claudel was likely the model.
Inception 1885/1889
image courtesy wikimedia commons

About Andrés + Mila in
The White Sky

In *The White Sky*, by John Caedan, two artists pursue an entanglement of the heart with everything at stake, made urgent by profound physical intimacy – love with sex, sex with love. They are not unquenchable – you will find them celebrating with family or unloading creative frustration to the sky on a deserted beach at dawn. However, the carnal hunger returns. Quickly.

In real life we do not see behind the closed bedroom door of mated couples. In *The White Sky* you can keep it that way, or not, as desired – the book respects both. While the story of *The White Sky* is complete in itself, the supplemental text (which is identical to the book you are reading now) provides their sexual encounters during their first month as a couple. It does not contain action of the main text.

Reading along in *The White Sky*, you will encounter this image with a page number. You may wish to open to that page and read of Andrés and Mila making love. The writing is explicit. You may need two bookmarkers!

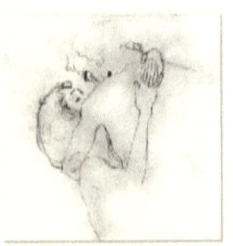

Gustav Klimt
"Two Lovers,"
1908

About this edition

Images:
Models, composition, and renders
by John Kirnan

Text font: EB Garamond
Designed by Georg Duffner, Octavio Pardo
for Google Fonts

Cover and Chapter font "Grechen Fuemen"
Designed by Robert Leuschke
For Google Fonts

Text block style:
Ragged right justification, non-hyphenated.
While writers are strictly advised to format
their texts with equal length lines,
I inquired if that included poetry.
No.

jjk

books by
J.J. Kirnan

Touch Me Again
Love in Bed
Jane Nineteen
Andres + Mila

jjkirnan.com
LoveInBed.com

books by
John Caedan

Eyes Full of Light and Laughter
SaraIRL
The Preludes
The White Sky

johncaedan.com

www.ingramcontent.com/pod-product-compliance
Lightning Source LLC
Chambersburg PA
CBHW020409150626
46554CB00012B/473